Fallin' for the Alpha of the Streets 2

K.L. Hall

Dedication

To Y.G.

Author Acknowledgments

Welcome back! You're probably ready to turn the page to jump right back into Pharaoh and Savannah's love story to see how it all pans out, right? Okay, okay! I won't take up too much of your time. I really hope that you've fallen in love with these characters just as much as I have. As of right now, this is the F-I-N-A-L-E *(I think)*. Anyway, on to the shout outs! Special thanks to you, the reader, for your continuous and unwavering support.
Penny and Allen.
Henry and Mae.
Henry and Dolly.
Gibbs.

All my love,
K.L. Hall

Fallin' for the Alpha of the Streets 2 Synopsis

Falling for Pharaoh Blackwell broke more than Savannah's boundaries; it broke her heart, too. She finds herself staring down the face of her tarnished FBI career for a man she had no business being with in the first place. In a perfect world, their lifestyles would've never allowed them to cross each other's paths. Now, she has to decide whether or not the badge clipped on her belt is worth losing her one chance at true love.

The hits that hurt the most are the ones you don't see coming. After losing the battle, Pharaoh will stop at nothing to win the war while fighting for his freedom. He never should've fallen for Savannah, but now that he has, one thing is for sure: he will *never* trust her again. When tragedy preys upon his close circle, he follows the trail of breadcrumbs that leads back to the most unexpected suspect. Pharaoh's only focus is to protect the people he loves from a looming street war against a rival gang.

There was a time when Elite thought that she'd found the kind of man she never dreamed of in "Rico." When she learns she's been sleeping with the enemy, she'll be forced to make a decision, one that could easily shred the last few pieces that are left of her heart. It's no secret that Frenchie needs to get his life together. Life and karma have teamed up to kick him while he's down. In order to get everything he wants, he'll have to show everyone around him that he can be the man they need him to be, but at what cost?

In the finale of this explosive series, the ties that bind between families and lovers will be tested. Everyone will experience the sweet insanity that comes from loving the ones they shouldn't. With Savannah and Pharaoh's worlds crumbling around them, they will be forced to either save their own lives or the love they share. They just may not make it out with both.

Epigraph

"You're allowed to miss the people who were bullets to you, but you're not allowed to let them shoot you again."

–Reyna Biddy

Previously in Fallin' for the Alpha of the Streets

The moment I stepped out of the car, I heard yelling. I quickly ran up to the door and tried to look inside. When I realized I couldn't see anything, I took a deep breath and opened the door. My eyes immediately widened at the sight of Shep tied up to a chair. He'd been severely beaten. One of his eyes was swollen shut, and there were bruises and lacerations on his face with caked up blood on them.

"Oh my God!" I yelled, then quickly covered my mouth.

Pharaoh and his cousin both looked up at me. One wore a smile, the other a frown. "I thought I told you to stay in the car," Pharaoh told me.

"What are you doing in here? Stop this shit right now!"

"Get the fuck out!" Frenchie yelled at me. "Let's hurry up and finish this nigga, P."

I watched Pharaoh turn away from me while pulling his gun out from behind his back. "Is this what you wanted, huh? To bring this side out of me, nigga? I treated you good, let you into my circle. This is how you repay me, by talkin' to the mothafuckin' Feds?"

Shep didn't say anything, and Frenchie drew back and pistol whipped him across the back of his head. As much as I knew I shouldn't have said anything, I couldn't stand by and watch them torture the man who was supposed to be my co-lead. I drew in a deep breath, knowing I would regret the words that were about to fly out of my mouth.

"Just tell him who you really are, Shep!" I yelled.

Pharaoh quickly turned his attention back to me. "Shep? How the fuck do you know this nigga?"

"I don't know her," Shep mumbled, trying to come to my defense.

"Move again, and I'll break your mothafuckin' face, nigga," Pharaoh said through gritted teeth.

"Yo, at this point, I don't give a fuck who the fuck this nigga is. It ain't gon' matter when they find the ashes of his fuckin' body in this bitch. Let's finish this nigga," Frenchie said.

Instead of listening to his cousin, Pharaoh turned his gun on me. I quickly stepped back and slowly raised my hands in the air. "How the fuck do you know this nigga?"

"I—I…"

"Don't you fuckin' lie to me, Savannah! Or I swear to God!"

"Pharaoh, please…" I whispered.

"I'm only going to ask you this once, aight? Are you or are you not a fuckin' informant?" he yelled.

"I'm not! I'm not an informant!"

"Don't lie to me! Don't you fuckin' lie to me!" he said, shoving the gun in Shep's mouth.

"Please don't!" I trembled.

"Tell me the truth right now, or I'll blow his fucking brains out right here, I swear to God!" he yelled.

My chest tightened as my mouth gaped open. I couldn't believe *what was about to come out. "I'm a special agent with the FBI," I said frantically with my trembling hands in the air. "And... Pharaoh Blackwell, you're under arrest."*

Chapter One

SAVANNAH

The worst part about falling in love with someone is knowing that there's going to come a day when one person is going to hurt the other.

"You have the right to remain silent..."

All I could hear was the dull beat of my heart as I stared into Pharaoh's fire-burning eyes. The way he looked at me broke my heart into a million pieces.

"Anything you say can and will be used against you in a court of law..."

The police sirens whined loudly in the background as the helicopter blades whirred rapidly in the distance. Pharaoh's gun cocked as he looked back at his cousin. "Run," he told him.

"What, nigga?"

"Get the fuck out of here!"

Frenchie looked at Pharaoh with a confused look on his face and then focused his eyes on me. "Fuckin' bitch," he grumbled and ran out the back of the warehouse.

"Pharaoh—put the gun down, please," I said calmly.

"If you gon' arrest me, then you gon' arrest me for killin' this mothafucka," he said as he drew his gun out of Shep's mouth and shot him three times at close range.

My lips parted as an ear-curdling scream blew out from deep within my lungs. I ran over to him as Pharaoh darted out of my sight. My knees hit the dusty pavement, and I pulled my phone out to call the ambulance. Within minutes, I could feel Shep's body losing heat. I wrapped my hands around the sides of his face. "I need to get you warm. Listen to me. Keep your eyes open, okay? The ambulance is on its way. Just stay with me!"

Tears filled the corners of my eyes as I rocked him from side to side and continued to talk to him until the paramedics rushed in. Shep was rushed to the hospital with life threatening injuries. I knew if he died, Pharaoh would have another charge over his head. As soon as I walked out of the warehouse alongside Shep on the stretcher, I saw Pharaoh being hauled into the back of a police car with cuffs around his wrists. My heart sunk to the floor, and my eyes soon followed. Pharaoh Blackwell was the trifecta: handsome, wealthy, and downright dangerous.

"Good work, McKinney," the chief said as he walked up beside me and patted my shoulder.

"T-thank you, sir." I nodded.

"I'm going to follow the car in to make sure that son of a bitch makes it down to the station. I'll see you there."

I stood back and watched the police car speed off with Pharaoh in tow. I had no idea where Frenchie was, but it seemed as if he'd dodged a bullet by evading the police.

MY TIME AT the Downtown Chicago police station was a blur. Their phones were ringing off the hook, while officers brought in more black and brown people than the precinct had space enough to hold. I passed by a few officers discussing cases behind the glass as I made my way into the break room to grab a cup of coffee. My lips brushed against the coffee cup, tasting the bitter, old coffee. I shuddered and lowered the cup when I saw the chief standing in the doorway.

"Everything alright, McKinney?"

"Yes, sir. Any word on Shep?"

"No, not yet."

"Did Blackwell get here safe and sound?" I asked.

"Sure did."

"Where's he being held?"

"The interview room at the end of the hallway. Why?"

"He shot my co-lead on this operation. I have some things I need to say to his ass."

He nodded. "Okay. Try not to go too hard on him."

"I'll try to remember that."

My hand gripped the coffee cup tightly while the other rested on the cold, steel doorknob. On the other side of the door was Pharaoh, who was slouched at the table with his wrists handcuffed in front of him. I walked in and closed the door behind me. My lungs drew in a deep breath as I watched my coffee steam in the cold air of the room.

"I'm sorry," I breathed out.

He cut his eyes at me. Although I had trouble meeting his eyes with my own, I couldn't help but notice his broad shoulders were spread wide and his hulking chest was heaving in and out with anger.

"Stay the fuck away from me."

"Just hear me out."

"Why should I?"

"Just let me explain, please. And don't worry, no one is watching us. You can speak freely."

"I ain't got shit to fuckin' say to you, and even if I did, you think I'd even trust a word that came out of your mouth?"

Guilt flooded over me. He had every right to feel the rage and embarrassment that burned through him. "I regret everything. All of it, okay? I never meant to hurt you."

"Get the fuck out of here, Savannah. For real."

"Everything I told you about me was real. I'm real. The only thing that's different about me is my occupation."

He frowned. "And that's one hell of a difference." He scoffed.

"You're right. You shouldn't trust me. Not after what I did."

"Cut the bullshit, Savannah. You knew exactly what you were doin' from the start. I fucked up and let you in. That's on me, but it's fuck you from here on out."

His tone was detached. Emotionless even. I could barely take the ice-cold demeanor he was dishing my way.

"Don't do this, please..."

"It's already been done."

"You think it didn't hurt me, too?"

"Do I look like I give a fuck if it hurt you? Look where the fuck I'm sitting, and then look at where you are."

"Just give me a chance to try and fix this, Pharaoh," I said, stepping closer to him.

He held up his calloused hand to stop me. "Stay the fuck over there."

I sighed. "Look, I might never get another chance to say this, but my heart beats literally only for you right now. I don't care about anything else."

His eyes bore into mine. Stifling silence hung in the room like rain clouds. All I could hear was the ticking of the clock to the same cadence as my fingertip against the side of my coffee cup. Minutes went by before I heard a response.

"Anything else you wanna get off your chest?" he asked.

"Pharaoh—"

"What the fuck do you want me to say, huh?" he growled.

"Say anything."

"How can I trust you when I don't even know who the fuck you are? Just be honest and tell me you were pretending this entire time. You ain't really fuck with a nigga. But let your boss know he got a real one. All that shit you was talkin' about celibacy and shit and even knowing who I was, you still bust that pussy open for me. They tell you to do that shit, too? Or was that all you?"

"Fuck you, Pharaoh."

He chuckled. "Yeah, aight." His voice was rugged and cold. "I'm a monster, right? Ain't that what they sayin' about me?"

My head shook from left to right. "I don't think that about you at all."

"Everybody actin' like they know me, because they know what I do, how I get my money, how I feed my family and my niggas, but they don't know shit about me. You was the closest person to me outside of Frenchie, and you said fuck all that for a fuckin' salary that I can make in a day. How the fuck you think that's supposed to make me feel?"

"Pharaoh, I'm so sorry. I—I never meant for it to go down this way. If I could take it all back, I would!"

His face burned with humiliation. "This is real life! Ain't no reset button on this shit. You make a mistake, you live with that shit. We just both gotta face the fact that you're not who the fuck I thought you were."

"Please, just—"

"My client doesn't have to say another word to you," Pharaoh's lawyer said as soon as he burst through the door.

My sad eyes flashed up toward his and then back at Pharaoh. Pharaoh wasn't an ex. He was a mixture between the past, present, and hopefully my future. He was something that started and hadn't stopped for me. At first, I was afraid to fall for him, then I found myself afraid that I would never be able to forget him.

"Now if you'll excuse me, I'd like to be alone with my client," he barked.

My teeth sunk into my bottom lip. "No problem," I mumbled as I removed myself from the room.

MY FEET SHUFFLED into the debriefing room where Agent Adams, the chief, and other members of the Chicago PD were gathered. The first thing that stood out to me was Pharaoh's name written in large capital letters on the dry erase board and his photos on the bulletin board.

"Agent McKinney, just the person I wanted to see."

"Chief?"

"You remember Agent Adams, right?"

"Yes... I see you got here fast," I said to her.

"What can I say? Good news travels fast."

I nodded quietly and shifted my eyes to the boxes of files on the front table.

"So, how do you feel?" she asked.

"What do you mean?"

"About catching the bad guy, McKinney."

"Oh," I said, rubbing the back of my neck. "I—I don't know. I guess it just doesn't feel real."

"Well, it's real. Come take a seat beside me. The chief is just about to start."

I followed her to the round table and plopped into the seat to her right. I didn't want to be there, let alone hear anything more about the success of Operation November and the capturing of Pharaoh Blackwell like he was some sort of rabid animal. As soon as the chief opened his mouth, I sunk further down into my seat.

"I want to thank everyone for convening here so quickly. Thanks to the undercover FBI agents with Operation November, I am proud to announce that Pharaoh Blackwell has been apprehended and placed in custody. We are now making arrangements to have him shipped off to a federal institution as he awaits sentencing. Now, Agent Adams, would you like to say a few words?"

She stood to her feet and nodded. "Of course. Just like he just said, thanks to the FBI agents from both the D.C. and Atlanta regions who took the initiative to help us bring down Blackwell. A special thanks to Agent Savannah McKinney for dropping a pin and calling it in. Because of that, we were able to apprehend Mr. Blackwell and will proceed in charging him with a laundry list of charges, including drug trafficking, gang affiliated-related killings, and money laundering. We are now in the process of freezing all of his assets, and as the chief said, getting him into federal custody as soon as possible."

Applause spread through the room like wildfire.

"Thank you to Chief Sanders for lending us a few of your men. Unfortunately, Agent Michael Shepard was shot while in his undercover role. He is now in the hospital with life-threatening injuries, but the doctors say he is expected to make a full recovery. Again, thank you all for your help in making America a better and safer place for us all."

PHARAOH

The hits that hurt the most are the ones you don't see coming. I was only four years old when I experienced my first one. It was when my mother left me on Big Mama's doorstep and disappeared from my life for good. Years later, the night Big Mama died became the beginning of the end. The moment they slapped those cuffs around my wrist, I knew shit was over for me. The only thing that kept playing on repeat inside my head was Savannah. When it came to her, my heart and mind were at odds, even after all she did to me. There wasn't a single time of the day where I didn't think about her. As much as I didn't want to admit it, I was nowhere near ready to quit her. On the other hand, there was a part of me that wished I would've shot her when I had the chance. I'd worked too fuckin' hard on my reputation to let anyone drag me through the mud.

"Yo, when are they gon' take these fuckin' cuffs off me?" I asked my lawyer as I looked him square in his eyes.

He sighed. "I'll see what I can do about that, but let's talk while we have a chance."

"What do you mean?"

"They are working overtime to get you shipped up and out of Chicago as soon as they can."

"For what? I don't even know what the fuck they holdin' me on."

"So far, they are trying to charge you with three counts of drug trafficking with the intent to distribute, one count of attempted murder on a federal officer, and two counts of money laundering."

"Fuck do you mean so far? There could be more?"

"If they bring any and all evidence they have against you, then yeah, it could be a hell of a lot more. Pharaoh, I wouldn't be doing my job if I didn't tell you that the odds of you beating this is—"

"Fuck the odds. I already beat 'em," I said, cutting him off. "Just get me the fuck out of here. I don't care if you have to make a deal with the devil himself."

"I'll see what I can do, okay? Until then, you just keep it together. Whatever they throw at you, you make sure you hold your fucking composure. Any wrong move and it's over. There are some things even I won't be able to find a loophole for."

I nodded. "It's just another situation. I'll come out on the other side just fine. Believe that."

He cracked a half smile. "Just hold on a little while longer, okay? I'm working for you. Remember that."

He patted my shoulder, grabbed his papers, and left me alone with the thoughts bouncing around in my head. For years, I'd dodged the Feds and all of their tricks, only to let a Fed in my circle and another in my bed. I was low. As down on my luck as I was, I would've taken a jail cell over a casket any day. Not even a second went by before Savannah's face popped into the forefront of my head. There were things that had been placed right in front of me that I chose not to see. I was ashamed to say French was right about her. It was more than her looks that got me. She had substance beneath the surface. Savannah was the type of woman who made me appreciate her mind just as much as I appreciated her body. I always thought she deserved more than me, but it turned out that she didn't deserve me at all. I made a vow to myself that from that day forward, I would keep a bulletproof vest around my heart. There was nothing more dangerous in this world than a man who didn't give a fuck.

Chapter Two

ELITE

I didn't think it was possible to feel the things I felt for another man besides Frenchie, but my entire world had been different since I'd fallen for Rico. The only problem was, I'd been calling him, and he hadn't been answering my calls.

"C'mon, pick up," I mumbled into the receiver.

As soon as I hung up, Frenchie burst through the front door looking like he'd seen a ghost. Beads of sweat slid down the sides of his face like it was the hottest day of the summer. "Frenchie, what the fuck are you doing bussin' up in here like the Feds? What's wrong?"

Instead of answering me, he started pacing the floor and mumbling underneath his breath. "Frenchie, hello? What the fuck is going on? Say something!"

"I can't fuckin' talk! I gotta think! I gotta fuckin' think!"

I jumped up from the couch and walked over to grab his shoulders. "Frenchie, just stop for a second, and tell me what the fuck is going on!" I yelled.

"They got P! They fuckin' got P!"

"What? Who got P?"

"The fuckin' feds, Elite!"

My eyes widened with terror. "Oh my God," I said, dropping my arms down to my sides.

"I can't believe they got this nigga! Man, fuck!" he yelled while continuing to pace the living room floor.

Tears swam out the corners of my eyes. "Who do you need me to call? Where's Riot? Where's Rico?"

He stopped as his eyes turned to steel. "Fuck that nigga

Rico, man! I hope Pharaoh killed his ass before they took my nigga away!"

My eyes gazed down to his shoes as they scuffed up the carpet. There were crimson specks all over them. I knew that couldn't have meant anything good. "Wait, what? What happened to Rico? Is he okay?" I asked frantically.

"That nigga was a fuckin' Fed this entire time, Elite! I had that mothafucka in my home! I caught a body with that mothafucka in the car with me!"

My heartrate quickened. "What the fuck did you just say, Frenchie?"

"He's a fuckin' rat! Him and that bitch Pharaoh was fuckin' with! They comin' for me! I know it! I gotta get the fuck out of here!"

My heart shattered into a million pieces for a million different reasons. I stumbled back to the couch and fell back against it while holding my chest. Everything I thought I wanted… everything I thought I was going to get had been set ablaze and turned to ash within seconds. It was if I'd just been woken up out of a fairytale only to realize none of it was real. I wanted so bad to call Frenchie a liar. To tell him he was wrong. Mistaken. But nothing would come out of my mouth. I was afraid that the second a word slipped out, I would choke and drown in my own tears.

"Elite."

I flashed my glassy eyes up at Frenchie. "Y-yeah?"

"Tell my babies I love them, but I can't fuckin' stay here. I can't be here right now until I know what's up."

Even though my eyes were set on him, I could almost see directly through him. As much as I should've been concerned about Frenchie's well-being since he was the father of my children, I couldn't help but to only think of Rico. I needed to know if what Frenchie said was true, and if it was, I was going to be sure I let him know he'd fucked with the wrong one.

I nodded at him. "I'll tell them."

MY HEELS CLICKED against the slick hospital floor on the way to see if what Frenchie said had merit. As soon as Frenchie left, I started trying to trace back to everything that had happened between Rico and me. It took me hours to find enough information to lead me to a hospital downtown that he might have been brought to. I rested my elbows on the top of the information desk and stared down the side of the nurse's head until she acknowledged me.

"How can I help you?" she asked.

"Yes, I called earlier and was told that you had a patient here named Rico."

"Do you have a last name?"

I shook my head. "N-no, I don't. But… he would've been brought in today with a possible gunshot wound. He's about six feet tall, beard, Caesar haircut, built body…"

"Let me see what we have in our records."

I listened to her nails click against the keyboard. "All we have here is a patient named Rico Saunders, but he's a nine-year-old boy. There's no one else here by the name Rico that's been admitted today."

I lowered my head in defeat. "Are you sure? Can you please check again?"

She clicked a few more buttons and then looked back up at me. "Nope, Rico Saunders is it. I'm sorry, but whoever you're looking for isn't here."

I slowly bobbed my head up and down. "Okay, thank you."

Feeling like my heart would never rest until I got answers, I sat in the waiting room and tried to collect my thoughts before dragging my ass back home as empty handed as I was when I left. I let out a long exhale as I buried my head in my hands. I didn't know how it was possible to have fallen for and gotten pregnant by a man, and I didn't even take the time to learn his last name. That's when I realized I was completely out of my element. Ending my relationship with Frenchie had driven me straight into the arms of a stranger who could unravel my entire family with the simple pull of a thread.

I slowly lifted my head and looked down the hallway as a stretcher with a patient on it came rolling down toward me. I stood to my feet, stretching my neck and straining my eyes to see who the patient was. That's when I saw his face. It was Rico. I quickly darted down the hallway and waited outside of the room until all the nurses left. My fingertips drew a line underneath the name written on the dry erase board inside his hospital room. Rico's real name was Michael Shepard.

My face screwed up as I looked at him with so much confusion and rage boiling in my heart. His eyes were closed and his heartbeat was low. He'd been badly beaten, but I could still tell it was him. His left arm was in a cast, and his ribs were bandaged. With my lips pressed together in a hard line, I stepped closer to the bed and leaned over him with tears in my eyes.

His eyes opened, and I backed away while wiping my eyes. "Elite?" he whispered.

"Who are you?" I whispered back.

He lowered his eyes and then tried to slowly sit up in the bed as best as he could. "Tell me what you've heard."

"Well, for starters, I realized today that I don't even know your last name as Rico, but then I also learned that none of that even matters because your real name is Michael Shepard."

"Elite, let me explain."

I threw my hand up to silence him. "Just tell me who you are. That's all I want to know."

My shoulders tensed. It amazed me how I could go from not wanting to be away from his touch to never wanting him to touch me again.

"I'm an undercover FBI agent from Atlanta."

I let out a loud breath as all the wind left my body at once. "This is a joke, right? Tell me this isn't real." When he didn't say anything, I nodded. "So it's true then."

"That depends on what you've heard."

"That you're a fed... You just said it yourself! Wow. Wow! I can't even believe any of this," I said, stepping further away from the bed.

"Elite! Just talk to me, please."

"Please, just let me go."

"I'm so, so sorry. I never meant for things to go the way they did."

"Was any of it real? Or were you playing me to get closer to French? Were you hoping that if you dicked me down good enough that I would just spill all his secrets? Is that what this was?"

"Nah, it wasn't like that. I swear."

"You think I believe anything you say? You're a liar. What do I even call you? Do I still call you Rico, or do you want to be called by your real name now? You're a stranger to me, nigga! A fuckin' liar and a stranger! You talked all that shit about Frenchie being the wrong nigga for me, and you're not even better! Yeah, Frenchie lied too, but at least I knew who the fuck he was!"

"I get that you're mad, but stop pushing me away, and let me help you," he said.

"Help me? You're the reason I'm standing in this mothafucka in the first place. Why the fuck couldn't you just stay away from me? Why'd you have to cross the line with me, huh? What, I wasn't broken enough, so you had to go and see how far I could bend before I break? Well congratulations, nigga. You shattered whatever the fuck was left of my raggedy ass heart!"

He sighed. "Elite, please—"

"You were supposed to be the beginning of a new chapter in my story, and now... you're just a page I want to rip out and burn. Do you know how much of a disappointment you are? I know I told you that you were a good guy, but I never expected this. I mean, were you ever going to tell me?"

"I tried to tell you when I was with you, but then I got the phone call, and Pharaoh and Frenchie tried to kill me. I thought I would never see you again. Can't you see that what you and I have is special? This is our chance to be together. No more secrets, no more lies, nothing. You can have all of me. Let me save you."

"Save me from what? More lying ass niggas like you? I swear to God I'm so sick of you niggas! Y'all either trying to save a bitch from a fucked-up nigga, or you are the fucked-up nigga!"

"I promise you, once you take that wall down that you're building, you'll be able to see that I'm the right one for you. It can be you and me against the world, Elite. We can start over together. You, me, the kids, and our baby," he told me.

"There is no you and me. I've decided not to go through with the pregnancy..."

His forehead creased. "What? Elite, why would you do that?"

"I can give you a million fuckin' reasons why I'm doing this. I'm pregnant with your baby, and I don't even know your real fuckin' name." The sound of my reality coming out of my mouth sounded just as harsh as it felt.

"It doesn't have to be as complicated as you're making it. You can still do the right thing."

I shook my head. He was delusional if he thought I was going to come anywhere near him. Being with Rico would put my entire life in jeopardy. In my opinion, it took a true psychopath to impersonate a fictional person for months and lie so much that they even forget the truth. "Look, don't make this harder than it already is, please. Just forget about me. About this. And just leave me the fuck alone."

"Forget about you? Elite, how can you honestly expect me to do that?"

"It's better this way. You stay on your side of the game, and I'll stay on mine."

"We can talk this out."

"There is no other way. It isn't up for debate. Whatever you thought we had or were ever going to have is over," I told him and stormed out of the room.

FRENCHIE

Forest green paint peeled on the front door of the trap house. I heard loud music bumping from someone's car stereo as they sped by, with the faint sounds of gunshots in the distance before I entered the house. The screen door creaked when I closed it, drowning out the faint moans I heard coming from the other room. Riot was in the living room sitting in the middle of two girls smoking a blunt, while they rubbed on each other's titties while two more girls counted money in the corner.

"Yo, what up, nigga?" he asked.

"Yo, let me holla at you real quick."

He outstretched his arms. "We good."

"Nah, alone," I told him and made my way into the kitchen.

I leaned against the wall and glanced up at the exposed

pipe above my head, waiting for him to come. I focused my attention on the line of empty liquor bottles on the bar, some with cigarette butts shoved inside them.

"What's the problem?" he asked, swinging into the kitchen.

I looked over my shoulders and then leaned into him. "P got caught up by the Feds, nigga."

"What?"

"They came after P. I know they are gon' come after me next. The fuckin' Feds been on us for months because of fuckin' Rico."

"That nigga was a rat?"

"Worse, a fuckin' Fed."

"What the fuck, man. We got bodies with that nigga and told him about the Millwood nigga. He about to tear us down," he said as he pushed his dreads out of his face.

"Maybe not. Pharaoh shot him."

"Did he kill 'em?"

"I don't know. I didn't stay around long enough to find out, nigga. If I had, both of us would've been in fuckin' cuffs."

"Nah, I feel you. Here," he said, passing me the blunt.

I pulled the smoke into my lungs and exhaled slowly. "That's not all, nigga."

"What else is there?"

"You know that bitch P was with that had his nose all wide open and shit?"

"What about her?" he asked.

"Fed."

His eyes widened. "Yo, what the fuck? This nigga P was fuckin' a Fed?"

"Yeah, it's verified."

"I need a drink."

"You?"

"I'll be right back."

I picked at the rippled wallpaper in the kitchen while puffing the blunt again. Riot came back and passed me a bottle of liquor. Without even looking at the label, I tossed some back straight out of the bottle. I slammed my fist into my chest as the burn from the cheap alcohol made its way into the pit of my stomach. "Goddamn that shit was strong."

The two of us stood in silence, thinking while passing the bottle back and forth. The wind whistled outside, making the house settle. Riot pulled his phone out of his pocket and answered it.

"Hello? Fuck you mean? Fuck, man! Aight, fine. Handle what you can, and then call me back," he said and hung up.

"Who the fuck was that?" I asked.

"Cops raided the storage unit on Wabash."

"Fuck! When is the next shipment coming in?"

"In about a week, and don't forget, we still need to secure a new connect within the next few weeks, or it might be back to knock off Gucci belts and Starter jackets for us, nigga."

"Well, we just gon' have to tighten up until then. With Pharaoh gone, you my second in command now."

"Bet. We gon' make it work."

I dapped him up and then my phone started vibrating. I slowly pulled it out and looked at the screen. The number was blocked, so I ignored it. I wasn't about to willingly hand myself over to the Feds and give them my whereabouts. My phone rang three more times before I answered it.

"Yo, who the fuck keep callin' this number?" I growled.

"I know what the fuck you did. MCF niggas gon' catch you slippin' on the block. Watch your back, nigga."

My eyebrows knitted together as I frowned. "Yo, who the fuck is this? I ain't scared of shit, bitch. BBG all day, hoe ass nigga!"

"Keep fuckin' talkin', and I'll send shots to where you lay your head at, nigga. You know what the fuck you owe me, and I want all my shit plus interest!" he said and hung up.

I slammed the phone down and glanced over at Riot. "Who the fuck was that?" he asked.

"Nobody. It was nothin'. Just niggas playin' on my fuckin'

phone."

"You sure?"

"Yeah, nigga. I told you it's nothin'. We just need to focus on making sure we continue to eat until we can get P out," I told him.

"Bet."

I nodded as I took one more swig of the liquor and turned to leave. As soon as I was alone in my car, I looked down at my phone. I'd known the streets my entire life. Niggas didn't play on the phone for no reason. I wasn't gon' spend the rest of my days looking over my shoulder. If anybody was gon' take me, they were gon' take me in blood. With my cousin behind bars and MCF and the Feds on my ass, survival was more than just breathing.

Chapter Three

SAVANNAH

The more days that passed by, the more I realized that Pharaoh was a mistake from the beginning. A handsome, stupid, earth-shattering mistake. As soon as I realized who he really was, a part of me knew we were going to end up saying goodbye to each other. I just never thought it would hurt so goddamn bad. I had a life before him. A life I'd forgotten. A life that once I remembered, I realized I never truly wanted to go back to. I missed his laugh. The way he smelled. Everything. No one knew how bad my lips ached for one more kiss. All I would have was a kaleidoscope of memories that would either comfort me or haunt me. I kept asking myself if it was possible that Pharaoh was the love of my life, but I just wasn't his.

I walked into Shep's dimly lit hospital room and walked directly over to the curtains to open them. He squinted as he waved me away. "Close them, McKinney."

"No! You're alive! That's a good thing! Why are you in here so depressed?"

"Just leave me in the dark."

"What's wrong?"

"Nothing," he grumbled.

I walked over to the side of his bed and peered down at him. "I know we haven't known each other for very long, but I was instrumental when it came down to saving your life, so level with me. Tell me what's wrong."

His nostrils flared then he let out a long sigh. "You remember when I gave you all that shit about being too close to Pharaoh?"

"Duty before love is what you told me," I reminded him.

"Yeah, well let's just say, I didn't take my own advice."

My eyes widened. "With who?"

"Is it important anymore?"

"Hell yeah, it's very important. Tell me."

"Elite." He huffed.

"Frenchie's girlfriend?"

He nodded. "Yeah, her. Go ahead and rub it in, or do whatever else you're gonna do."

"Why didn't you tell me about you and Elite?"

"It might sound stupid to say, but I—I felt like I was in love," he confessed.

I nodded. "Me too."

"Then you know how hard it is to get out once you've fallen in."

"Yeah, I do. I don't know though, maybe it's time that we both just really try and move on."

"Maybe that would be easier if she wasn't pregnant," he told me.

"She's what?"

"Yeah."

"Is it—yours?"

"Yeah."

"Oh my fucking God, Shep! Are you crazy?"

"I know, I know. It wasn't planned."

"What the fuck are you going to do?"

"There's nothing I can do."

"What do you mean?"

"Now that she knows who I am, she said she doesn't want to keep it."

I lowered my head. "Oh, I'm-I'm sorry."

He shrugged one arm. "Maybe it's for the best... That's a bad thing to say, huh?"

"Kinda, but I get it."

"I mean... it was never going to work, right? We were like

teenagers from the opposite side of the tracks. We were doomed before we even got the chance to really begin."

I shrugged. "I just wish things would've turned out differently. Like, maybe if we would've met years earlier before he went into the streets and I went into law enforcement. We could've been great. We could've made it. We all could've."

He shook his head. "You know what's crazy to me? I don't understand how the ones that everyone knows need saving the most are the ones who never want to be saved."

"Maybe she doesn't need to be saved, Shep. Maybe she just needs to be loved."

He shrugged his good arm. "Is now the part when you tell me something from a Disney movie like 'do what's in your heart' or something like that?"

"No."

"Good, because if I did what was in my heart, I'd rip these tubes away from my body, track her down, and never let her go again," he confessed.

I thought I was the only one who had fallen prey to Pharaoh's ways, but Shep was in the same boat with me, and we were drowning. "The good thing is, we managed before them, and we'd find a way to do it after them."

"I hope you're right," he told me.

"Yeah, me too."

PHARAOH

I was all alone in my jail cell and stuck in my feelings. All I wanted to do was drink, smoke, or fuck my pain away. Savannah taught a nigga that I was right to never trust a bitch. As much as every atom in my body wanted to hate her, I couldn't shake the feelings she gave me out of my system. She was my bit of good within all the bad. She was who I went to when I needed an escape. In the blink of an eye, all that shit was gone.

After my last conversation with Savannah, I was transferred to booking and then placed in a cell until they could finalize my transfer to an out of state prison. Every day that went by, it felt like the concrete walls were getting closer and closer. My hands gripped the side of the stainless-steel sink then turned on the faucet. I splashed some cold water on my face and looked at my reflection in the mirror. I spent most days trying not to have a run-in with no sucker ass MCF inmates or guards. Any other time I had I spent trying to push against the darkness inside my head if I ever did have a run-in. I knew the cloudy way I viewed the world would probably destroy me one day, but I had to turn my heart into steel if I was going to survive another day inside the iron box.

My feet paced the hard concrete floor in the pair of uncomfortable shoes they gave me until the guard walked up to my cell and rattled the bars like I was a fuckin' monkey in a cage.

"Let's go, Blackwell. Time to meet with your lawyer," he said.

All I could do was fantasize about snapping his neck as soon as he got within arm's length of me. I quietly followed him down the maze of hallways and corridors until I was put in a secluded room to wait for my lawyer.

He entered quickly and set his briefcase down on the table. "How are you doing, Pharaoh?"

"You mean besides the fact that they got me caged behind iron bars like a mothafuckin' animal?" I answered back.

"I'm working and pulling as many strings as I can, and I do have an update for you."

"Let's hear it."

"Well, they want to sentence you to life."

"Life?" I yelled.

"But they are willing to reduce it to twenty years max if you take a plea."

"Fuck that! I'm not takin' no deal until they can show me exactly what evidence they got to hold me on all these fuckin' charges they got on me."

"You can either entertain the idea of taking the plea deal or take it to trial, but we both know that you'd be gambling with your life if you did that. We all know that you're guilty; it's just my job to try and lessen the time. Either way you spin it, you're looking at facing time. Unless..."

"Unless, what?" I asked.

"Do you think you can get the FBI agent you had ties with to drop any evidence they're holding against you?"

"Hold up, how you know I had ties to her?"

"I heard your conversation the day they brought you into custody."

I shifted uncomfortably in my seat and nodded.

"But they've frozen all of your assets, so we wouldn't have any way to try and offer her money in exchange for her silence."

"Fuck her. I don't want to speak about her. If it's money you need, then that's not a problem. I'm a millionaire, fuck all that other shit. I just need you to get me the fuck out of here. I'm gon' lose it on one of these mothafuckas in here. Even in a jail cell, people are still gunning for me."

"Alphas and betas don't mix. You just gotta hold on through all the hate, the trash talk, all of it. They want to sentence you to life, Pharaoh. With as much money as you have, you can't afford a fuck up in here."

I sighed. As put together as I was on the outside, I was a damaged nigga with abandonment issues and years full of resentment on the inside. My blood was raging all the time. If I couldn't take my rage out on the people I wanted to, I was going to end up doing it to one of the inmates, and it wasn't gon' be nothin' nice. My mother left when I was four years old, and I'd been a raging bull ever since. It didn't help that I never knew my father. I was driven into the streets by my own personal demons, and I didn't do well when I wasn't in control.

FRENCHIE

The fan whirred overhead as I lay across Bria's bed. As much as I didn't need any more kids, I wasn't going to not be there for Bria if she was carrying my twins. She lay propped up against some pillows while she ashed my blunt and passed it back to me.

"You gon' tell me what's wrong with you now?" she asked

me.

"No."

"Why not?"

"I don't fuckin' feel like talkin' about it."

"Fine."

"You know what I do want to talk about though?"

"What?"

"Why the fuck you went to Elite to tell her you were pregnant?"

"Because I knew you were lyin' to me when you told me you would leave her, so I handled it myself."

"You ain't handle shit. If anything, you made shit worse. Now I can't stay in my own house."

"You can just stay here like you been doing, but instead of doin' it every now and then, you can do it all the time," she told me.

I shook my head. "Nah. I'm not doin' all that until I know if them kids you got inside you are really mine."

"Stop playin' with me, Frenchie! You know damn well you were blowing my fuckin' back out at least a few times a week."

"And I always wore a fuckin' condom with you."

"Oh, so it's cool for you to fuck Elite raw all the time, but not me, when I been ridin' ya dick for months now?"

I shook my head. "You talkin' wild right now."

Bria was childish. She was quick to get a thorn in her side whenever I mentioned Elite as if she didn't know her place in my life. She was a fool if she really thought I would ever leave Elite for her. "You really trippin' right now. I'm about to get up out of here," I told her.

I sat up from the bed and put my blunt out. "Wait!" she yelled.

"Nah, I'm good. I ain't come over here for this shit. A nigga already stressed enough."

"Baby, I'm sorry," she said, coming after me. "I don't want

to argue either."

"Goddamn, Bria." I sighed.

"You know I got what you need to calm you down," she said, softening her voice.

She walked over to her dresser and pulled out a small bag of coke. "Here, it'll make you feel better, baby."

I caught the small bag in my hand and quickly dug in my pocket for a piece of money. "No, sniff it off my belly," she told me.

"What?"

"You heard me."

Bria lifted up her shirt, exposing her naked breasts and baby bump. She laid flat against the bed, and I crawled on top of her. I quickly tapped out a small line of coke against her skin and then sniffed it off. Once I was done, I leaned my head back then forward to kiss it.

"I love you, French. We... love you," she said, placing my hand on her stomach.

Bria was the type of chick who I could fuck from the front because she was gorgeous or hit from the back because she had a nice ass too. I couldn't make up my damn mind. I wanted my family back, but I also wanted some pussy. As soon as the drugs started flowing through my system, I slid her panties off and buried myself between her legs.

She spread them wide for me, and I started slowly licking her clit in slow circles. "Mmm, shit." She purred.

As soon as I started to lick faster, my phone vibrated in my pocket. Thinking it could have something to do with Pharaoh, I stopped to answer it.

"Hello?" I said, putting the phone up to my ear.

"You ready to listen now, mothafucka?"

"Yo, who the fuck is this?" I growled.

"I told you what the fuck I wanted when I called the last time, didn't I?"

"I don't know what the fuck you talkin' about. Now stop callin' my mothafuckin' phone or it's gon' be a problem," I warned the anonymous caller on the other end.

"A problem, huh? I'll make sure you can never go back to your fuckin' set, bitch, and if you run, I'll make sure there's not a city you're safe in, nigga."

My fists balled as my chest pounded with rage. "I'm callin' your bluff, bitch. What's good? Pussy ass nigga." I snarled and hung up.

"Who was that?" Bria asked.

"Some bitch ass MCF nigga keep callin' me. I don't even know how the nigga got my number."

"MCF? Why the fuck are they callin' you?"

"I don't know. Some bullshit."

Bria rolled her eyes. "Didn't sound like."

"Why the fuck you all in my phone call? Damn!"

"Sorry!"

"I got my mothafuckin' middle finger held high to them niggas. Fuck them!" I told her.

"Mmm."

I looked at her while scratching my beard. "Fuck is up with you?"

"What are you talking about?"

"You actin' funny."

She sucked her teeth. "Fuck you mean? How?"

"You heard what I said, Bria."

"Are you seriously going to argue with me again?"

"Nah, you know what. I'm out."

She yelled my name at my back as I grabbed my shit and left through the front door. It could've been the drugs causing my paranoia, but somethin' didn't feel right. It was the second phone call I'd gotten about the money and drugs I stole the night Big City was killed. At first, I didn't pay it any mind, but the second phone call had me livid. I had to make sure that I kept my gun in arm's reach to be ready for any MCF nigga that came my way.

Chapter Four

SAVANNAH

"Today's the day, McKinney," the chief said to me.

"What's happening today, sir?"

"Blackwell is getting transferred right out of the state of Illinois."

"Do you know where they're sending him?"

"Federal prison out in Texas. You know the district attorney offered him a plea? Fuckin' twenty years isn't enough."

I swallowed hard. "Do you think he's going to take it?"

"I hope not. I want his ass to suffer through months of trial just so the jury can convict him and ship him off for life."

"You really don't like him, do you?" I asked. "Any particular reason why?"

"It was drug dealing pieces of scum like him that flooded my neighborhood back home when I was a kid. My mother got addicted to that shit, and it took her from me when I was only eleven. I vowed right then and there that I wasn't going to let that shit destroy another family if I could help it. Getting people like him off the street are the only way to stop this fuckin' drug epidemic."

He spoke with such passion in opposition to the man that my heart did backflips for anytime I saw him. It was so weird that two people could have totally different viewpoints on the same person. As much as I didn't want to see Pharaoh get shipped away, I knew I had to do what was in my heart.

"With all due respect, Chief, I understand your views, but while I was undercover, I didn't witness Mr. Blackwell assault or shoot Agent Shepard, so I can't testify against him."

"Don't you fuckin' do this to me, McKinney. I need your statement that you saw him physically assault Agent Shepard! Without any written statements from Agent Shepard since he's still in the hospital, and his doctors are refusing to allow him to make any statements until he's completely healed, they'll let Blackwell get out on bond. Your statement is the only thing we have that we can hold him to!"

"I'm sorry, sir, but I'm not going to go onto the stand and say something that I didn't see happen. I don't know how he got beat. I didn't even see him shoot him. I ran in after he'd been shot, and Blackwell fled. I dropped the pin once I saw Shep in the condition he was in and called the ambulance," I told him.

"Mother fuck!" he yelled. "Why would you choose now of all times to go soft, McKinney? I had such high hopes for you, but now I know that it was a mistake bringing you onto this team."

I frowned. "He's in custody. Isn't that what you wanted?"

"Excuse me?"

Instead of responding, I turned on my heels to leave. "If you walk out of that door, you might as well leave your badge on the table," he said to my back.

I turned back around to look at him, then looked down at my badge. Without a second thought, I unclipped it and dropped it on the table.

IT TOOK ANOTHER few days for Pharaoh to get released, but once I was sure he was out, all I wanted to do was be in his presence. I sat in my living room and called his phone repeatedly. I figured he hit decline every time out of spite. I couldn't blame him. I called back three more times before he answered.

"What?"

"Can we talk?" I asked quickly.

"We don't have shit to talk about. I said what I had to say to you at the police station."

"Can you please just tell me where you are? I'll meet you

anywhere you want, Pharaoh. Please. There are just some things I need to get off my chest. Once I do that, then I'll leave you alone for good, I promise."

I heard him let out an aggravated sigh, and then nothing. "H-hello?" I asked.

"It's my niece's birthday. I'm at the Play Zone downtown for her party, and this is where I'll be for the next few hours. If you make it while I'm here, then cool; if not, that's it. I'm done."

"I'll be there," I assured him and hung up.

THERE WERE DOZENS of clothes spread out all over my bed as I paced the floor, trying to decide what to wear. I was nervous as if I was going on a job interview or something. Once I decided on what to wear, I made sure my curls were extra bouncy, and I put on the perfume that I knew drove him wild. If my words didn't convince him of how much he needed me, I knew my looks would.

I sat in the back seat of the Uber while I waited for him to come outside. Just the look of him standing with his hoodie close to his chest and his hands in his pockets, made me pinch my thighs together. I quickly got out of the car and walked over to him. "Hey..."

He turned to look at me with a straight face and didn't return the gesture of telling me hello.

"Thank you," I told him.

"For what?"

"Talking to me again."

"I ain't said shit yet," he said.

"Okay..."

"Start talkin'. I'm missin' the party."

"Sorry, I just... there are so many things I want to say to you that I don't know where to begin. I mean, I've been thinking about what I was going to say to you whenever I had the opportunity to see you again. When'd you get out on bond?"

"Not too long ago, but something tells me you already knew that."

"I told you I would fix it."

"Excuse me?"

"I told them I wasn't going to testify, Pharaoh. Without my statement that I actually saw you shoot or assault Shep, they couldn't continue to hold you. That's how you were able to get bonded out."

"You want a congratulations or somethin'? You think I owe you somethin' for that shit?"

"No, I'm not saying that. I'm saying that I get it. I have trust issues, too."

He let out a hearty laugh. "You talkin' to me about mothafuckin' trust issues, and look what you did to me! I have a reputation to uphold, and you got me out here lookin' crazy as fuck. I just don't need the distraction. You're a danger to my well-being, Savannah. I can't fuck with that, and I can't fuck with you."

"So that's it?" I asked breathlessly.

"You were expectin' somethin' other than the truth?" he bit out.

"I don't know what I was expecting, honestly." I shrugged.

"Let me just say this. This city is too fuckin' small for the both of us, and I ain't goin' nowhere."

Ignoring his attempt to send me running out of the city, I changed the subject. "I know that now, maybe we aren't destined to be anything other than two souls who passed in the night, but I can't stop thinking about every *what if* scenario after scenario playing in my head... I can't help but wonder if I'll ever hear you tell me that you love me, *too*..."

His eyes were stormy with anger. "What?"

"Yeah, Pharaoh. I—I love you." My chest stuttered as I reached out to grab his arm. He pushed my hand away.

"I don't love you, Savannah."

My heart shattered like a sheet of glass hitting the floor. I felt like the wind had been knocked out of me. Everything around me starting spinning. I hadn't felt heartbreak like that since I was in high school.

With stinging eyes, I parted my lips and said, "Just don't ever tell me I didn't mean anything to you, because we both know that'd be a lie."

"I should've killed you when I had the chance after all you put me through. I could've been in jail for life because of you! Then how everybody around me gon' eat, huh? The fact that you're standing here in front of me should tell you that I cared about your ass. If not, wouldn't have been this much talkin' between us," he told me.

"Do you think you'll ever change your mind?"

He shook his head. "I gotta get back inside."

"Okay, I—"

"Leave, Savannah. Leave this fuckin' city, and never come back. I don't want shit to do with you."

Pharaoh had made it crystal clear that he didn't want me around him, no less the entire state of Illinois. Feeling defeated, I watched him walk back into the building while I stood with my feet planted in the cement underneath me. My brain kept telling me to move, but nothing happened. I stood paralyzed in heartbreak for five minutes straight until I turned around and went back around the corner to call myself a ride to my apartment and then the train station. One thing was for sure, no matter where I went, I would be leaving my heart in Chicago.

ELITE

Pink and gold confetti scattered across the tables at my baby girl's birthday party. I looked around at the large pink balloons floating in the air, the streamers taped to the wall, and the brightly wrapped birthday presents on the gift table. Amidst

the sea of kids running in and out of the play areas while screaming with cheer, I saw my Imani. She had on a pink and purple
tutu with a crown on top of her braids, with gold crown beads
on the ends of her hair. She was gorgeous. I'd never been more
proud to be her mother than I was in that moment.

"Imani, come here for a second," I said, waving over to
her.

She bounced over to me with a wide grin on her face.
"Yes, Mommy?"

"Are you enjoying your birthday party, Princess Imani?"

"Yes!" She squealed. Every muscle in her body was dan-
cing around. She was excited about her birthday party, which
made me happy. I looked over at the bucket of melting Neapol-
itan ice cream on the table and decided it would soon be time
for cake and ice cream.

"You can play for a little bit longer, but it'll be time for
cake and ice cream soon, and then you can open all your presents, okay?"

"Okay, Mommy!"

"Now, gimme kiss," I said, poking out my lips.

Imani stood on her tiptoes and gave me a kiss on the lips.
I playfully swatted her butt as she ran off to go play some more
with her friends and cousins. I went ahead and pulled the cake
out of the box and started putting the candles in them when
Frenchie walked over and swiped some icing off the cake with
his finger and put it in his mouth.

"Don't do that, Frenchie! You're going to mess up her
cake!"

"She ain't gon' notice."

"Whatever," I said, rolling my eyes.

While most of the parents sat around chatting and eating, I walked around and started trying to clean up a few of the
tables so I wouldn't have much to do by the time the party was
over. I glanced up at Imani who was diving in and out of the
ball pit and smiled. Looking at all the plates of half-eaten pizza

started to make me sick. Soon a wave of morning sickness rolled through my body. I gripped my stomach as my eyes quickly scanned the room for the nearest bathroom. As soon as I was done, I walked out of the stall and stood face to face with my mother.

"Is there something you want to tell me, Elite?" she asked.

I sighed as I stepped to the side and went to the sink to wash my hands and splash some water in my mouth. "I'm sure you already know."

"Are you pregnant again?"

I looked at her through the mirror and nodded. "I'm pregnant, Mama."

"Oh my God, Elite! I don't know whether to hug you or smack you."

"Look, I don't want to talk about this right now, okay? So can you just save whatever speech you were planning on giving me for another time. I have to get back in there. It's time for cake and ice cream."

"Elite!" she yelled after me.

"Later, Mama!"

I pushed past the door and walked back out into the chaos of Imani's birthday party. I looked all around the room filled with screaming children and didn't see mine. Without thinking twice about it, I went back over to her cake, lit the birthday candles, and looked around for her again. "Imani!" I said, calling out her name.

"Where is she?" I asked, walking over to Frenchie.

"Fuck you mean, where is she?"

"I can't find her, French!"

"I'm sure she's around here somewhere."

I took Paxton from him, and we both walked around, calling out Imani's name, while the other parents looked too. Each minute that went by felt like days. My skin crawled with fear as I forced down another sick feeling in my stomach. I handed Paxton off to my mother. "Let's go check outside."

I ran behind Frenchie, and Pharaoh was hot on my heels.

By the time we'd gotten to the edge of the sidewalk, we saw two men shoving Imani into the back of a truck and speeding off down the road. My throat clenched as pain gripped at my chest. I let out all the screams I'd been biting back since the moment I couldn't find her.

I watched Frenchie take off down the road, chasing the truck on foot. He pulled out his gun and aimed it. Just before he was about to pull the trigger, Pharaoh grabbed his arm, and he shot in the air.

Pharaoh pulled the gun away from his hand and pulled Frenchie down to the ground. I dropped down to my knees in shock. "I—I feel like I can't breathe," I said, clawing at my chest.

"Somebody fuckin' call 9-1-1!" someone yelled out.

All I remembered after that moment was hearing ear-curdling screams that sounded like they were coming from far away, but in fact were coming out of my mouth. Frenchie ran over to me and pulled me off the ground.

"Elite, come back inside, baby. We gon' figure this out."

"What did you do? Huh? I know it was you! It had to be you!" I said, wind milling my arms at him.

He stepped away to block my blows as Pharaoh came and pulled me away from him.

"Tell me I'm wrong!" I yelled.

"I didn't do shit."

My eyes swam with tears. "I know you had something to do with it!" I yelled, pounding my fists into his tattooed chest.

His brows snapped together. "Yo, Elite. Chill out. Let's just get you back inside. We'll figure all of this out."

We slowly walked back inside, and all eyes were on us. One look into my mother's eyes brought fresh tears to mine. The room smelled like just-blown-out matches that my baby didn't have the chance to blow out. There were a pile of her tickets that she wouldn't get the chance to cash in, and birthday presents that she would maybe never get to open. My soul was crushed.

Pharaoh, the girl that Frenchie told me was a Fed, and my

mother made sure the guests and their children were escorted out. My mother took Paxton to her house, while Pharaoh, Frenchie, and the girl hovered around me in a semi-circle.

"Elite..." Frenchie called my name.

I glanced up at him without saying a word. "Please say something... anything," he begged.

"Just tell me what you did, Frenchie." I sniffled.

Both Pharaoh and Frenchie looked back at the girl, and Pharaoh escorted her out of the room. I had no interest in knowing why she was there. The only thing on my mind was getting my little girl back.

"I already told you I didn't do shit."

I darted my eyes over to all the glossy wrapping paper on the gift table and shook my head. I could feel a weight settling onto my heart. "If you're going to continue to sit here and lie to me, then I'm done."

He frowned. "What the fuck you mean, Elite?"

My temples throbbed with rage. "I mean that I'm done trying for you. I'm done trying with you. I'm done. I'm fuckin' done. I don't care what you gotta do or who the fuck you gotta kill, but you better bring the other half of my heart back to me, Frenchie."

Chapter Five

FRENCHIE

"Everybody just calm down, aight? Don't worry, Elite. We gon' find out what they want, and we gon' get Mani back," Pharaoh told us both.

My stomach knotted. "I already know what they want."

"What?"

"I knew you had something to do with this shit!" Elite yelled.

"What the fuck is going on, French?" Pharaoh asked me.

"A payment for a debt."

"What debt?" Elite asked.

My chest caved as I leaned against the booth across from where Elite was sitting. For months, I'd let the guilt of leaving Big City for dead torment me. The MCF nigga who kept callin' me showed me that he wasn't playing around, and because I didn't take him seriously, I'd single handedly put my baby girl in harm's way. As much as I didn't want to, it was time that I came clean.

"I've done some shit that I can never take back," I mumbled.

Pharaoh narrowed his eyes at me. "What did you do, Frenchie?"

"The night Big City died… I was there."

I focused my attention on Elite's trembling hands as I started recalling the events of the night. "I remember it was cold out. Not gloves and a skully cold, but cold nonetheless. I wanted to get into something. We both did. I'd just gotten out of custody, and I was tired of waitin' on P to put me on. I was all over the place that night. You ever just get a feeling that you can't shake? It's like you know somethin' is wrong or about to go wrong, but you're in too deep to stop it? That's exactly what that entire night felt like. I asked Big City to ride out with me, and we spent the first two hours riding, smoking, and listening to music. We turned down a back street over in Terror Town, and that's when I saw him. I ain't know who the fuck he was or what he had on him, but I knew he was gon' be my target.

We parked the car a half a block away and got out. Within seconds, I cocked my gun and ran up on him, putting the steel to the side of his head and told him to give me every fuckin' thing he had on him. It wasn't until I saw the tattoo on his trembling hand that I realized he was an MCF nigga. I ain't think nothin' of the shit. If anything, I thought it would be a win-win situation for me. I'd get whatever he had on him, and I'd put another one of those pussy ass niggas six feet under.

I watched him pull a few hundred dollar bills out of his pocket and then fell to the ground. He was scared. I pushed him over to Big City, who patted him down and pulled his car keys out of his other pocket, then tossed them to me. I pressed the unlock button and saw the car across the street light up like it was Christmas time. We marched him over to the car and popped the trunk. I remember my pupils turning into green dollar signs when my eyes landed on the two duffel bags filled with cash and the three kilos of coke. *Jackpot,* I thought to myself.

Big City held him while I ran down and got the car and put everything into my trunk. Just before we got back into the car to ride off, I fired my gun at the nigga, and his body dropped. I revved up the engine while Big City ran around to the passenger side. Before his hand could grip the door handle, shots rang out like the fuckin' Fourth of July. I watched the surprised look on his face when my foot slammed on the gas and I sped off. I watched the reaper take his soul from my rearview mirror, and I ain't been right since," I admitted.

Elite looked at me with tears in her eyes. "So that's where the drugs came from and-and the money to buy my fuckin' engagement ring? You did all that with stolen money, nigga? Did you not think that somebody was gon' come lookin' for their drugs and their money?"

I shook my head. "At the time, I didn't give a fuck. All I was thinkin' about was feedin' my goddamn family, aight? So nah, I wasn't thinkin' about nobody comin' after me."

"And you thought that leaving Big City's fuckin' body there wouldn't point back to the rest of BBG?" Pharaoh asked, shooting me a venomous look.

"I know I fucked up, aight? I can own that. I gotta live with that shit for the rest of my life."

"And if you don't find a way to bring my baby home safe and sound, I swear to God I'll never forgive you," Elite said abrasively.

As soon as those words fell off her lips, my phone started ringing. I looked at the screen and knew exactly who it was. "It's them," I said aloud.

"Put that shit on speaker," Pharaoh said.

I pressed the green button and then put the phone on speaker. "Hello..."

"Didn't I tell you not to fuck with me, French? If we can't get you, then we'll get your people."

"Tell me exactly what you want, and I'll do whatever I gotta do to make sure you get it. Just don't touch a single hair on my daughter's head, or all bets are off," I growled.

"Oh, so now it finally sounds like I've gotten your attention. You stole two million dollars from me and three kilos of my product, which means you now owe me three million and four kilos."

I swallowed hard. "When."

"I'll let you know the time and place. You just work on gettin' me what I asked for, and don't try no slick shit either, mothafucka," he said and hung up.

I lowered my hand back down to my side and looked at both Pharaoh and Elite. She popped up from her seat and pushed me. "I fuckin' hate you for this shit! I swear to God the second my daughter is back in my arms, you're dead to me, Frenchie! Dead!" she yelled and stormed out.

PHARAOH

Anger rolled through me as I watched Elite leave, then I turned back to Frenchie. He'd rested his heavy head in his hands, while my entire body stood stiff. Everybody I cared about kept lying to me. The only thing I could do was turn my emotions completely off and submerge everything into the streets.

"I'm sorry I lied to you, fam," he told me.

"Don't fuckin' talk to me, nigga."

"What the fuck you want me to do now? I can't change the past, P!"

"Why the fuck would you lie to me? Nah, that ain't what real family do to each other. Big City's blood is on your hands, nigga. Remember that."

"You don't think I fuckin' know that shit? It haunts me every single fuckin' day! No matter what I do, I can't get the fuckin' devil to stop riding me."

"You don't act like you know shit!"

Frenchie sighed and shook his head. "Why'd you stop me from shooting the truck?" he asked.

"One, because you have two strikes already, and two, because your baby girl was in there. The last thing you needed was for one of the bullets to hit her."

He lowered his head and bobbed it up and down. "I didn't even think of that. All I could see was red."

"That's your problem, Frenchie. You don't fuckin' think, ever! You gotta stop movin' the way that you've been movin', French. I been told you about this shit! The moment you robbed that nigga, you put a target on your back and ours, too! I swear to God if you weren't family, I'd kill you!"

I used to think we had the same blood running through our veins, but finding out that Frenchie was responsible for Big City's death changed our family dynamic forever. We were at war with each other, our enemies, and ourselves.

Frenchie puffed out his chest as darkness crossed his eyes. "I can't believe this nigga is playin' with my fuckin' family. He must got a death wish."

"Do you got a name for this mothafucka?"

He tapped his foot nervously against the floor. "No. All I know is he's wrapped up with MCF. He never drops a name, but it seems like he knows any and everything about me."

"What about the MCF nigga you shot? Did you kill 'em?"

"Didn't stop to check." He shrugged.

"If he ain't dead, then there's your answer right there. He probably was able to identify you."

"Still doesn't explain how they got my number."

"You said you left Big City there. They probably took that nigga's phone and followed the breadcrumbs right back to you."

"Man, fuck!" he yelled loudly.

I let out an exasperated sigh and reached out to pat his shoulder. "Fuck what happened, aight? We gon' bring her home. I refuse to believe it's going to end like this."

He nodded. "I'll go crazy if anything happens to her."

As mad as I was at him, I knew he was probably hurting the most out of all of us. The last thing any of us needed was for Frenchie to fall off the deep end. We needed to figure out how to take down everybody who was threatening to strip away what I'd built. It was the second time that I'd been caught off guard by the enemy lurking in the shadows. Both the Feds and the MCF gang had been waiting for a vulnerable moment to pounce, and they did. Even though they might've had me in their trap, I planned to go down swinging to the very end.

ELITE

It had been three long, nerve-wracking, excruciatingly painful days without Imani.

There was a pile of dishes in the sink, and the entire lower half of the house smelled like old takeout pizza. I'd been waiting by the phone as if I was waiting on a miracle to happen or for someone to just drop her back off on my doorstep and tell me how much of a misunderstanding the entire thing was. All I did was wait. Cry and wait.

As soon as I started the dishwasher, I picked Paxton up from his swing and held him close to me while smelling the top of his head. "C'mon, baby boy. It's time for Mommy to give you a bath."

During the entire bath, Paxton sat there laughing and clapping while splashing around the iridescent soap bubbles in the water. I was happy he was so young and had no idea what was going on in our lives at the time. After Paxton's bath, I rocked him to sleep and placed him inside his crib. As soon as I closed to door to his room, I locked eyes on Imani's door. There was a sign hanging around the doorknob that read "The Princess is in."

Against my better judgment, I turned the cold doorknob. I walked into her room and suddenly felt breathless. I could still smell her presence. Everything looked exactly how she'd left it the day of her birthday party. I ran my hand across the top of her dresser, then glanced over at her bed. The sequined T-shirt she wanted to wear on her birthday was still laying across her narrow, twin-sized bed. Beside it was her growing stuffed animal collection. I walked over and picked up Mr. Bear, her favorite one of them all, and brushed the soft fur across my face.

I squeezed my eyes shut as tears overflowed from the sides. My baby girl's room was empty. I heard a car door slam outside and walked over to her small window with pink curtains to look outside. Frenchie's car was there, and I rolled my eyes. I knew that Imani was just as much Frenchie's as she was mine, but I didn't care. All I could see was rage when I thought about him or even heard his name. She didn't need him in her life. None of us did.

I turned back around to put her bear back where she'd left it and noticed that my mother had placed all of her unopened birthday presents inside her room in a pile in the corner. I glanced up at the ceiling, trying to stop the tears. All I could ask was why it had to be us. Why it had to be my daughter. If I could've traded places with her, I would've in a heartbeat.

"Elite," I heard Frenchie's voice say from the doorway.

"What the fuck are you doing in this house, Frenchie?"

"She's my daughter, too. I miss her just as much as you do."

"Yeah, the one who you put in this mess in the first place. I swear, everything you touch you fuckin' ruin!"

He stepped inside Imani's bedroom and sat on the edge of her pastel pink comforter. "Look, I know you're upset, and you have every right to be, but please stop shutting me out."

I drew in a deep breath and smelled the scent of the new

box of crayons sitting on top of her toy bin filled with dolls and dress-up clothes.

"I meant what I said, Frenchie. You crossed the line. It's fuck you for life. You're selfish! You don't know how to love anybody but yourself."

He sprang to his feet like an opened jack in the box and grabbed both of my wrists, squeezing them tight. "You can't know what love is when you're brought up in so much hate. My mother died at the hands of my father. My family is broken. My childhood was fucked. What the fuck do you want me to do? I can't help that I turned out like this. I can't change who the fuck I am!"

"I see that now," I said, jerking away from his grasp.

"The monster under my bed was my own fuckin' daddy. A killer raised me!" he yelled as his chest rose and fell with rapid breaths. "I'm tryin' to be better than that, but you ain't lettin' me."

"I gave you chances on top of chances to be a good man and a good fuckin' father. It's not my fault you waited too long to try and cash in on them! Look at us, French! We are falling apart at the seams!"

"Just trust me. I know what I'm dealin' wit'."

I shook my head. "When are you going to stop lying to yourself? No, you don't. Now please, just get out!"

"I'm not leaving, Elite."

"If you're not going to leave, then I will."

"You can't just leave our home."

"That's exactly my point. This isn't our home anymore."

"Elite, please don't leave me. Not like this. I need you now more than ever."

"You always need me, Frenchie! Every single time you fuckin' fall down, who is always there to pick your grown ass back up? Me! But it's my turn to be down now. It's my turn to fuckin' fall apart, and you can't save me!" I said, touching my hand to my heart.

Without waiting for his response, I brushed past him and went into Paxton's room to start packing more clothes into his diaper bag. Frenchie followed behind me and watched me from the doorway.

"Don't take my son from me, Elite."

"I would never stop you from seeing your son, but we can't stay here anymore, Frenchie. We just can't. I'll be at my mom's house with him."

He walked in and picked up Paxton from his crib and laid him against his chest. "Just let me say goodbye first."

"Fine. I'll be downstairs loading up the car," I told him.

TWO HOURS LATER, I was sitting in my childhood bedroom watching Paxton's chest rise and fall as he slept through all the drama that had just went down between his father and me. My eyes darted over to the door when I heard a gentle knock.

"Come in," I said.

The door opened, and my mother walked in. "Everything okay?"

"I don't feel like talkin', Mama."

"I just came to say one thing."

"Look, I don't want to talk about Imani, French, this pregnancy, or anything, okay? If you aren't helping me get my daughter back faster, then I don't need the speech."

"Let me ask you this one thing, and I'll leave you alone about why it is that you really showed up here."

I rubbed my temples. "What is it, Mama?"

"Would you be proud of the man Paxton became if he turned out exactly like Frenchie?"

My forehead creased. By the look on my face, she knew my answer. "No," I said, shaking my head.

"Then why would you even entertain the idea of marrying him in this state?"

I sat there, struggling not to scream at her. The last thing I wanted to do was see Frenchie, let alone talk about him. There hadn't been an engagement ring on my finger in weeks, so I didn't know why the hell she was still talking about a wedding. "I'm not, Mama. The wedding is off. I'm done with him, for good this time."

"For good, huh? Elite, I bet you've said that more times than you can remember."

"Well, it's the truth this time," I told her while picking lint from my sleeve.

"Do you still think about him?" she asked.

My shoulders sagged while I darted my eyes over at Paxton's sleeping body. "Morning, noon, and night," I admitted.

"Then that's where your heart is, Elite. You can't change that, no matter how much you may want to. The sooner you stop lying to yourself, the better off you will be. If you want to be mad at him, then fine. Be mad. Just don't force yourself to feel a way about him when you know deep down you still care."

She took in a sharp breath as the air around me went thin. I was completely submerged in my grief. As right as she was, I wasn't in the right headspace to hear any of it. Tears welled in the corners of my eyes. "I don't know if I'm strong enough to do this, Mama. What if I don't get my baby girl back?"

She walked over and sat on the edge of the bed beside me. I knew she felt my pain since Imani was her grandchild, but I didn't think anyone could fully understand what I was going through. I was trapped in my own personal hell with no way to escape.

"Why don't you come to church with me on Sunday."

"I can't remember the last time I stepped foot inside a church."

"That's exactly why you need to go. You'll feel better once you're there. I promise."

SUNDAY CAME AROUND, and I rested my back against the cold wooden pew beside my mother. When the service started, I grabbed the bible from the shelf of the back of the pew in front of me and turned to Psalms chapter thirty-four, verse eighteen.

"The Lord is close to the brokenhearted and saves those who are crushed in spirit. Amen." The entire congregation read aloud.

I took my seat, and the pew creaked. The pastor began to preach about God's glory and mercy and how he could heal those going through pain, but I didn't feel it. I didn't feel anything but grief, pain, and anger that he was supposed to be washing away. As the choir sang their own rendition of Kirk Franklin's "The Storm is Over Now," the pastor invited everyone to come up to the front of the sanctuary for a prayer of healing. I quickly passed Paxton to my mother and walked up to the altar.

My head tilted back as I tried not to let the waterworks flow from my eyes by looking out of the stained-glass window. As soon as I felt the pastor rest his hand on my shoulders, I fell to my knees and lost it. Everyone inside the church knew that I was more than a broken woman; my soul had been completely shattered.

The pastor began to pray over me and my family, while voices from the congregation mumbled in agreement during his prayer. I needed all of the help I could get.

Chapter Six

SAVANNAH

Hard rain pelted down on the roof of the hospital as I sat in the chair across from Shep's bed. "It's really coming down out there, huh?" he said, sparking conversation.

"Mmhm, yeah."

"What's wrong with you?"

I cast my gaze down to my squeaky wet shoes. "When's the last time you talked to Elite?"

"She came by when I was first admitted to the hospital. I haven't heard from her since. I've tried calling and texting, but after the millionth time, I decided I'd just give her time and see if she'd come around."

"So you don't know what happened a little over a week ago?"

"What? Is she okay?" he asked.

"Her daughter was kidnapped at her birthday party."

"What!"

I lowered my head. "Yeah."

"How do you know all of this?"

"I went to see Pharaoh."

"So that's why she hasn't been returning my calls."

"Yeah."

"Do they know who is behind it?"

"They might. Pharaoh kicked me out before I got to hear anything."

He leaned against the side of his bed and ran his hand down his beard. "Shit. Now I want to talk to her even more."

"So that's why when we go meet with the chief today, you

can't give any statement."

"Excuse me?" he asked, scrunching up his forehead.

"They want your statement to set him behind bars, but you can't do it, Shep. Not now. They need their family back. I know you care about Elite, so you have to respect that."

"So you want me to go in there and lie like you did?"

I sighed. "I didn't lie. I just didn't tell the complete truth."

"Exactly, because you know damn well that you were there when he pulled the trigger on me."

"Please, Shep."

"If, and that means if I do this, then I'm not doing this for you; it's for Elite."

"Fine."

"Fine," he repeated. "All over him?" Shep asked me as I helped him put his things in the back seat of the car I'd rented.

"Must I remind you of a certain baby mama love triangle you have going on yourself?" I asked him.

He threw up his good arm in surrender. "Chill."

I closed the car door and started the engine. "I don't even know why I agreed to meet with the chief. I meant I was done when I left my badge on the table."

"So are you really done?"

"Looks that way." I shrugged.

The rest of the car ride was silent until we pulled into the parking lot of the police station the chief was meeting us at. It was his last day in the city, and he wanted to see Shep and me before he left. As soon as the precinct door opened, my ears buzzed from the dozens of conversations that were going on at the same time. I followed behind Shep as he walked into the vacant room at the end of the hallway that had doubled as the chief's out of town office.

"You wanted to see us, Chief?" he asked.

"Agent Shepard, how are you feeling?"

"Coming along."

"I'm glad you came, Agent McKinney," he told me.

I nodded without a response and took a seat across the

table from him.

"It's been a hellish few months, hasn't it, Shep?"

"Yes, sir, it has."

"What should be an open-and-shut case has now gotten messy. We've been playing this game of cat and mouse with Blackwell for what seems like forever. And to be honest, I blame you both for a botched crackdown. Because of McKinney's refusal to write a statement and testify, and without yours Shep, he got out on bond."

"I'm sorry that I got shot and was in the hospital for over a week, sir."

I shifted uncomfortably as I listened to the heat behind his voice when he spoke. "What happened to you being a stickler for the rules?" I asked the chief.

"I'm not going over this with you again, McKinney. All Operation November was supposed to be was an investigation without all bullshit. I wanted the bad guy behind bars and to move the fuck on, but because of the two people closest to the entire thing, the bad guy is still out here on the fuckin' streets!" he yelled.

The room fell silent as all three of us were boiling hot with rage for three completely different reasons. "What do you need from me, Chief?" Shep asked.

I cut my eyes at him as the chief smiled. "I need every bit of information you have against him so we can get the judge to revoke his bond, and we can get him back in custody where he should be."

"With all due respect, sir. I would be lying to you if I told you things weren't a blur from the assault. As far as all the other information I brought to you, you can do what you want with it."

"We already have. We raided the storage unit they were stashing drugs in. It took a while, but we got to the bottom of whose name the unit was being rented under, and we're still in the process of freezing all of his assets."

"What'd you find in the unit?" Shep asked.

"I'm expecting the full report sometime today with a detailed list of what they found."

Shep bobbed his head up and down. "Okay."

"I just need you to give a statement of every bit of information you've shared with me over these past few months, and everything you can pull together from the assault, even if you have to exaggerate some parts."

"Excuse me?" He frowned.

"You know what I mean, Shep. Add in a few more details to make sure that once we nail his ass to the wall, he'll stay there for the rest of his worthless life."

I frowned and bit down hard on my bottom lip to keep from cussing the chief completely out. As much as I knew I should've gotten up and left, I needed to make sure Shep stuck to his word. Instead of responding back, Shep pushed his chair back and stood to his feet.

"Let's go, Savannah," he told me.

I cracked a slight smile and stood beside him, then we turned to walk toward the door.

"If you're not going to help me, then get the fuck out of my office!" the chief yelled at our backs.

"I got out of the hospital for that shit?" Shep asked while rubbing the back of his neck.

"This is exactly why I'm done with all of this shit. I stood right in his face and told him that I didn't see anything, and he wanted me to give a written statement and get up on the stand to testify against Pharaoh."

"Wow."

"Still think you're on the right side of the law?" I asked.

"You think you can talk to Pharaoh to see if he knows anything about the kidnapping yet?"

"I doubt he'd tell me."

"Try anyway." He nudged me. "I'll keep trying to call Elite."

The phone rang three times before Pharaoh answered. "You shouldn't be callin' me."

"Just let me help you," I told him.

"Nah, you good. This is family business."

"Listen, you don't have to forgive me, speak to me after this, whatever... Just let me help you."

"The cops can't get involved with this, aight? This is street shit. Ain't no rules to follow."

"If you haven't noticed, I haven't been too good at sticking to the rules, especially not when it comes to you."

"Just leave it alone, Savannah," he said and hung up on me.

FRENCHIE

On the outside, I looked like nothing in my life had changed. I was still out there smokin', drinkin' and fuckin' whoever the fuck I wanted. On the inside, I was going crazy without Imani, Paxton, and Elite in my life. There was this homesickness in my heart for them, and the pain was too much to deal with every day, so I submerged my pain in weed, liquor, and pussy.

Riot and I were sitting in a booth in the back of the Waffle House after the club let out. As soon as the waitress put my plate on the table, I barely came up for air before I cleaned my plate. "Yo, lemme get another waffle," I told our waitress.

"Damn, nigga. Slow your greedy ass down. Fuck you so hungry for?"

"Gotta soak up some of this liquor," I told him.

He bit into his bacon, egg, and cheese sandwich without saying another word to me. After I devoured my second waffle, I got up to go to the bathroom. I walked down the hallway and pushed the door open, when it was quickly pushed back in my direction.

"Yo, what the fuck, nigga!" the nigga standing behind the door yelled.

"My bad, nigga. I ain't know you was back there. Chill."

"Be more careful next time, mothafucka."

"Chill the fuck out, nigga. I told you I ain't know your ass was fuckin' back there," I growled.

He looked me in the eyes and cocked his head to the side. "Wait a minute, I know you."

"No the fuck you don't. Get the fuck out my way. I gotta take a piss."

I brushed past him and walked over to the urinal to handle my business. After I washed my hands and pushed the door open, I saw him leaning against the wall. I grilled him while looking him up and down. From the look on his face, I could tell that nigga was gon' be a problem. I planted my feet firmly to the ground and balled up my fists at my side. "Fuck are you still doin' here, nigga?"

"I told you, I know who the fuck you are."

I quickly lifted up my shirt, brandishing my gun. "You don't want no smoke, nigga. Get the fuck outta my face," I told him.

He rushed me back into the bathroom door, grabbing me by my coat. I quickly shoved him off me, and his back slammed into the urinal. I pulled my gun out and aimed it at him before he had the chance to regain his balance. "Who the fuck are you, nigga?"

"I'm the nigga you robbed and shot!"

My eyes widened. I didn't know if I'd killed him or not the night that I shot him, but I for damn sure didn't expect to come face to face with him ever again. "Well you better get the fuck out my face before I shoot your ass again, nigga."

"You sure about that? Xae wants the drugs and the money you stole from me."

"Xae? Who the fuck is Xae?"

"The nigga that stole your daughter, and if you don't give back what's his, then he'll be the nigga that *killed* your daughter," he warned.

I tightened my grip around the gun, anxious to pull the trigger. "Don't say shit else to me, or I'll feed your ass a fuckin' bullet," I promised him.

He chuckled. "Nigga, you really out here thinkin' you on top when you losin'."

"Fuck you. You don't know shit about me, nigga."

"I know a whole lot about you; just ask your bitch, Bria. She made sure that nigga Xae knew you real well."

My body stood frozen as I replayed Bria's name falling off his tongue over and over in my head. When I blinked, he took off running away. I slowly lowered the gun and shook my head. There was no way Bria was playing me, but then again, I only came around to lay my head and lay the pipe. I tucked my gun back in my pants and walked back out to the booth where Riot was still sitting.

"Nigga, what the fuck you was back there doin'? Takin' a

shit?"

"No, nigga," I fumed.

"Good, because I know I'm a nasty nigga, but that back there is nasty, nasty."

"I gotta go," I told him.

"Where you goin'?"

"To talk to Bria."

I hopped in my car and sped out of the parking lot. What should have been a fifteen-minute drive, took minutes. My foot pressed the gas pedal as hard as it could, and I was at Bria's apartment door before I knew it. "Open the door before I break this mothafucka down!" I yelled while banging my fist.

I quickly heard the door unlock and watched it swing open. Bria stood there looking at me with an attitude written across her face. "Nigga, are you crazy? You tryna have my fuckin' neighbors call the cops on my ass?" she snapped.

I pushed past her shoulder and walked into her apartment. She slammed the door behind her and then turned to look at me. "What's wrong with you, Frenchie?"

"I'm gon' ask you this one time and one time only. Who the fuck is Xae?"

I could tell I'd caught her off guard as soon as her eyes widened. "Wh-what?"

"You heard what the fuck I said."

"You remember that night your ass was out at the club, poppin' pills and bottles and shit? You remember when you saw me and my girls? Yeah, I peeped you out easy. You loud, Frenchie. Loudest nigga in the club, and you ain't even have to say shit to me."

"Fuck is you sayin', Bria?"

"I walked right into your area and got you drunk enough so that when we left, you wouldn't notice the niggas followin' us all the way back to my crib. They got your plates and your address, nigga. Yeah, I fucked you. I liked it, too, but I'm a ride or die bitch for my nigga," she said, clicking her tongue.

The tables suddenly turned, leaving me to be the one who was surprised. "Xae," I told her.

"Yup. That's my baby. He say get 'em, I say got 'em. At first, all they were gon' do was rob you, but before that shit got set into place, you fucked around and stole his shit."

I shook my head in disbelief. "I knew those fuckin' twins you were tryna pin on me weren't mine."

"You really think I would waste my time getting' pregnant by a nigga like you? Please!" she said, snorting with disgust.

"So why the fuck would you go to my girl and lie about carryin' my fuckin' seeds when you wasn't?"

She shrugged effortlessly. "What can I say? I'm a shit starter. You spent all this time pillow talkin' with me while sniffin' coke off these pretty ass titties, telling me everything. How the fuck you think they know you got three other kids by two different bitches?"

"That ain't hard information to find out."

"Yeah, especially not from you. I got you out here lookin' silly, nigga. I been playin' you for months. You were the perfect target."

"Fuck are you talkin' about?"

"Please, I been knew about Elite. I know where she works, what she looks like, where your kid goes to school. How you think I found her on Instagram in the first place? I knew she was tired of you, and all I had to do was play on that shit. You can look in her eyes and see that."

I grabbed her by her throat and gave it a tight squeeze. "Who is playin' who now, bitch?" I said through gritted teeth.

"If you kill me, you'll never see your fuckin' daughter again. I'm the only one who can take you to where she's at."

"Tell me where the fuck she is before I snap your mothafuckin' neck right off your shoulders, Bria," I said, pushing her back against the wall.

"You remember the nigga you robbed and tried to kill? That's Xae's brother, and believe me, that nigga don't play about his family," she said, rubbing her belly.

I drew back and punched a hole in the wall right beside her head and she screamed. "Bitch, I'll kill him and his whole fuckin' family if he harms a hair on my daughter's head. Now tell me where the fuck she is."

Tears welled in her eyes while she shook her head slightly as I talked. It took everything in me not to slam her ass through the wall. I staggered back a few steps and then turned for the door. My chest was heaving in and out as rage pumped through my veins. I was an animal. I could barely explain the messed-up thoughts in my head. All I knew was one thing: I had murder on my mothafuckin' mind.

PHARAOH

Frenchie showed up at my house, banging on my front door at four o'clock in the morning. I kept my gun in arm's length and almost shot his ass as soon as I opened the door. "What the fuck are you doin' here, nigga?"

"I'm goin' crazy, P."

"What the fuck is goin' on?"

He walked in and sat on the couch with his hands clasped together. "I got the devil in me. I can feel him in my head, under my skin. That nigga runnin' through my veins, man."

My forehead creased. I didn't know if he was really trying to tell me something, or if he just needed someone to vent to. "Yo, I know you wanna get your daughter back, and I feel you, but don't do nothin' stupid."

"Too late. I can't stop it. I ain't got shit but murder on my mothafuckin' mind, nigga. You feel me? I'm fuckin' dreamin' of committing a fuckin' homicide."

"Where the fuck did you just come from, French?" I asked with concern written across my face.

K.L. HALL

"Bitch been playin' me the whole time. First she fucked up my shit with Elite by tellin' her she was carryin' my baby when she wasn't."

"You ain't fuck her?" I asked.

"Yeah, I did, but I knew I never hit that shit raw, and I'd been doin' it for months."

"How she try to play you then?"

"I found out that the twins she's carrying aren't mine. She been settin' me up so those MCF niggas could rob me, but before it went down, I hit that MCF nigga up for his drugs and his money. The nigga I robbed and shot ain't dead. He's the brother of the head of the MCF Gang."

"So that's who has Imani?"

"Yeah, some nigga named Xae. I'm tryna go get them niggas tonight."

"Yo, you gotta chill. If you don't, you gon' fuck up somethin' and we may never see Imani again," I warned him.

He looked at me and shook his head. "I can't handle losing my baby girl. I'll go fucking crazy," he said with teardrops in his eyes. "They might as well lock me up now, because once I get my hands on them MCF niggas, I swear to God I'll carve my fuckin' name in each of their faces. Goddamn, my head is so fucked up right now I don't know even know myself."

He let out a slight laugh. Even still, I could hear the undertone pain in it. Frenchie was torn between the love he had for his daughter and his unquenchable thirst for revenge. I watched him swipe a tear from his eye.

"I ain't come here to fuckin' cry, nigga. I came here to figure out a plan to get my kid back. I need all hittas on deck and ready to spill a whole lot of MCF blood on sight."

"Try to get some sleep, aight? We'll send any information you have out to the hittas first thing in the morning. We gon' do whatever it takes, French."

He nodded. "I'll do this if it kills me."

I WOKE UP the next morning and went downstairs to see Frenchie sitting on the couch with a cloud of smoke hovering above his head. "How long you been up?" I asked him.

"Never went to sleep," he admitted.

"You good?"

"Got another phone call this morning. I guess Bria went back and told that nigga that I threatened to kill her if she didn't tell me where my daughter was at."

"What they say?"

He unlocked his phone and played the voicemail on speaker. "Unless you wanna see your fuckin' daughter's face on a T-shirt, you better give me what the fuck I want. I ain't no amateur with this shit, nigga. I'm a murderer. When I call, you fuckin' answer like my bitch. Next time I call you, I want my shit COD, nigga. Cash on demand."

He put the phone down, and I shook my head. He passed the blunt to me, and I declined. "I missed the call when I was in the bathroom," he said, letting his arms dangle helplessly at his sides.

"I'ma call Riot right now and tell 'em to let everybody know what's up. If it's a war they want, it's a war they'll fuckin' get." I shrugged.

Riot was standing on my front porch within thirty minutes. He walked over to dap up Frenchie and I as he sat down. "Nigga, you look like shit," he told Frenchie.

"Shit is gettin' worse. I gotta stay high all day just to make it through to the next twenty-four hours."

"Tell me what the fuck is going on."

Frenchie spent the next fifteen minutes catching Riot up on the entire truth about his involvement with Big City's death. The three of us sat in silence until Riot spoke up. "How much do you have left of what you stole?" he asked.

Frenchie shrugged. "Two kilos and maybe seven-hundred and fifty stacks."

"Out of two million dollars?" I yelled, clenching my fists.

"I got caught up, and I'm payin' that shit back now, just not the way I thought I would be," he said miserably.

"So what we gon' do?" Riot asked.

"I've been workin' on tryna figure that out. That nigga said he wants three million and four kilos, but since the Feds raided the storage unit on Wabash, I don't know what the fuck I'm gon' do," Frenchie said.

I could feel my temples starting to throb. As smart as the Feds were, I was smarter. They thought they had me shook by trying to freeze all of my assets. Once I started making real money in the game, I made sure that I paid for everything in cash so I could put anybody's name down on whatever I wanted. I'd never been the type of nigga to put all my eggs in one basket, so I had enough drugs and money to last me a while. As soon as I got out, I picked up my cash from my stash spots that no one knew about. I never spent all my money in one place. Splurged here and there, but never to excess, but if I didn't find a new connect before I ran out, then we would all be fucked. Before I got locked up, I was supposed to fly out to New York to meet with someone, but with all Frenchie's drama and the Feds breathin' down my neck, I couldn't move how I wanted to.

"I can get the bricks and however much you need," I said, slowly unclenching my fists.

"I can throw in five-hundred thousand," Riot told him.

"For real? Thank you, nigga."

"Pockets might be hurt for a lil' while, but I'll do anything to make sure you get your family back. I can't even imagine what you goin' through right now. Shit make me wanna go to my baby mama house right now and hug my sons for the rest of my life."

Frenchie nodded. "All I wanted to do was just be able to ball out when I wanted to. Wake up Elite and tell her let's take the kids and go to Paris on a Tuesday type shit. I'm not a nine-to-five nigga, and I never will be, but if I gotta flip burgers or bricks to get her back, I'll do that shit."

Listening to French and Riot made me happy that I didn't have any kids. I'd never entertained the idea of being a father before Savannah, but since we were over, I had no intentions of making it come to fruition with anyone else. The way my heart was set up, I had no intention on lettin' another female get close to me again. My life turned me into a fuckin' monster. The streets turned me into a beast.

"So what about you, P? I never stopped to ask you how you was doin' in all this shit," Frenchie said.

"What you mean?"

He shook his head. "Nigga, you know what I mean. I told you to watch that bitch. What was her name?"

"I don't want to talk about her," I said, cutting him off.

"I'm just sayin'. You be out here thinkin' you know shit all the time. When I spotted her, I knew she was different, and not in a good way. In the snake way. Now look at you."

"Yeah, look at me. I'm out of jail, charges are pending, but if they don't come back with shit, then they gotta drop everything. I'm just waitin' on a call from my lawyer to tell me I can finally wake up from this nightmare."

"So you done with her?" Riot asked.

"Hell yeah I'm done with her ass. Wouldn't you be if you were me?"

"I mean, I'd probably try and fuck her one more time just for the fuck of it to get her ass sprung off the dick all over again and then break that bitch heart."

I glanced over at Frenchie, and he nodded.

"I'm not tryna go nowhere near her ass."

"I never got to ask you why the fuck she showed up at Imani's birthday party in the first place."

"She kept blowin' me up and told me that she wanted to talk, so I told her pull up and she did."

"What she want?" Riot asked.

"To apologize and shit."

"I bet her ass is sorry."

"Then after the whole shit that went down at the party, she hit my phone talkin' about she wanna help get her back."

"Tell that bitch to mind her fuckin' business," Frenchie grunted.

"I did."

"None of this sounds crazy to y'all?" Riot asked.

"What?"

"So you mean to tell me the day the Fed shows up at Imani's party, she gets taken, and now she wanna help you get her back? Sound like a setup to me."

"What you mean?"

"What if she's in on the whole thing, and this is just all some shit to get you to fuck with her again?"

I shook my head. "Nah. She not that coldblooded."

Riot shrugged. "Shit, I don't know. I'm high. I stick to what I said at the beginning, just go back to fuck her."

"That's what you would do, huh."

"Hell yeah. I'd be fuckin' that bitch in my Gucci flip-flops with my hat turned to the back," he joked.

Frenchie and I both shook our heads. "You wild."

"Trust me. All these fine ass women want is a nigga to discipline 'em. Think about it. Half of 'em got daddy issues anyway, right? Why you think they be callin' niggas daddy with a 'z' or papi? And why the fuck you think we get turned on by that shit? It's in our nature, blood."

"He got a point there."

"So you just never even entertained the idea of settlin'

down?" I asked.

"Nigga, settlin'? I got too many hoes waiting in line to throw they pussy at me or drop down on they knees like my nigga Kaepernick. I'd be a fool to pass that up. But shit, if you catch me on a good day, I might fuck around and get married tomorrow and divorce that bitch in a week. I don't know. I've never been one for commitment, nigga. You can't tell me God put more women on earth than men for us to be fuckin' one and only one. People don't call me Riot for nothin'. That monogamy shit is foreign to me."

I shook my head. "Nah, you just a hoe, nigga."

Frenchie chuckled. "I thought I was bad. You gon' be the type of nigga to get some crazy ass incurable disease that ain't nobody ever heard of before."

"Fuck that. I stay strapped. I got a lifetime supply of condoms, you feel me? Ain't nobody about to catch me slippin'."

"Fuck you mean, nigga? You got two sons!" I reminded him.

He sucked his teeth. "Yeah, but that's different. I got twins with the only female I ever trusted."

"So why not be with her?" Frenchie asked.

"Man, Karma and I... that shit would probably never work. What we got goin' on right now keeps us both happy. I get to go out and do what I want, when I want, she gets to live in a spot that I pay for, put groceries in, and drive a car that I bought her. We both got what we wanted out of the deal. As long as my kids are good, we good."

"I hear that, but the longer Elite stays gone, the more I start to miss shit I was never even worried about before."

"What's that shit Big Mama used to say? You never—"

"Miss a good thing 'til it's gone," he said, cutting me off.

"Yeah, that."

"See, look at you over here all heart shot up, bleedin' and shit, when you could be out here not givin' a fuck like me."

"Ain't no gettin' through to this nigga," I said, shaking my head.

"Aye, I'm a dog nigga, and the bitches love it," he said, followed by a bark.

I let out a loud exhale while Frenchie stood to his feet and dapped me up. "Look, I'm about to get up out of here."

"You sure you good?" I asked him.

"Shit, I guess I'm about to head out too," Riot said, following suit.

I dapped Riot up and walked them both to the door. Once Riot stepped outside, Frenchie turned to me. "Thank you, for everything," he told me.

"You don't got to thank me."

"I know, but I want to."

"You good. You family," I assured him.

"And as true as that may be, you will never, ever see me cry again."

Chapter Seven

ELITE

Fantasia's "Free Yourself" was playing through the built-in speakers in the ceiling as my scissors snipped my client's hair into a bob. It was the first time I'd been back to work since Imani had been taken. My mother thought it would do me some good to get back to doing what I loved, but it wasn't the same. The entire salon smelled like a mix of burnt hair and eucalyptus mint shampoo, but the entire place was packed. As soon as my chair was empty, I pulled my other client out from underneath the dryer while my shampoo girl had my next client at the shampoo bowl.

Just after I started to part her hair into sections so that I could blow it out, I felt a sharp pain shoot through my stomach. "Ouch," I said, bending over.

"Are you okay?" she asked me over the loud blowing of the hair dryer.

I left my client sitting in the chair and hurried to the bathroom. As soon as I locked the stall door, I pulled down my panties and saw blood. My heartrate quickened as I rested the back of my head against the door and closed my eyes. I knew exactly what was happening. All the stress of losing Imani caused me to lose my baby. After I was calm enough to show my face back out in the open, I went over to the front desk where Nique was sitting.

"Hey, can you see if you can get one of the other master stylists to take my clients. I have to leave."

"What's wrong?"

"I have to go to the hospital."

"Hospital? Elite, what's wrong? You're scaring me."

"I think I-I'm having a miscarriage," I whispered in her ear.

LATER THAT EVENING, I was laying on the couch watching Paxton as he slept in his swing. As much as I didn't want to be around Frenchie, I didn't want to be around my mother even more. After the doctors at the hospital confirmed my miscarriage, I was discharged and decided to come back home. I was torn between feeling sad and feeling like a weight had been lifted off my shoulders. I had been too busy grieving the loss of Imani, that I'd neglected to protect the new life growing inside of me. Although I'd told Michael that I planned to get an abortion, after everything that happened at Imani's party, I was paralyzed with the thought of her being taken. Nobody needed to know that Frenchie wasn't the father. I was going to take whatever Michael and I had between us to the grave.

Paxton stirred in his swing when Frenchie's keys started jingling in the lock. As soon as he came through the door and saw me, his eyes lit up. "Hey," he said.

"Hi."

"What made you come back?"

I bit down on my bottom lip. Truth was, I didn't have an answer for him, at least not one I thought was good enough. "I don't know." I shrugged.

"Well, I'm glad you're here. I have something to tell you."

I uncurled my body from the fetal position and sat up straight. "What is it?"

"You remember the bitch that sent you all that shit on Instagram tellin' you I was her baby daddy?"

I rolled my eyes. "I don't want to talk about that shit, Frenchie."

"Nah, hear me out. The bitch came clean and told me she lied about the whole thing. Those not my twins she's carryin'."

"What do you want me to say, Frenchie? Congratulations?"

"You don't believe me?"

"I don't know what I believe anymore, Frenchie." I could feel myself getting mad all over again, and I didn't need that added to the emotional roller coaster I was already on.

"I'm tellin' you the truth. She told me she knows where Imani is."

My eyes bulged out of their sockets as I jumped to my feet. "What? Why would somebody fuckin' play like that, huh? What the fuck weirdo shit is that bitch on? How the fuck would she know where the fuck my daughter is?"

He shook his head. "Bitch was playin' my ass for months."

"What?"

"She fuckin' some MCF nigga named Xae and was tryna get me set up to get robbed after they figured out who I was, I guess. I don't know. All I know is I'm going to fix this."

I shook my head. "I'm sorry for not believing you, but it doesn't change anything between us."

"Why you act like you can't see that I'm fucked up over this shit?" he asked me.

"I'm hurting, too," I told him.

"You sure about that?"

I frowned. "Why would you even say something like that to me?"

"I'm sayin', we supposed to be family, and you up and left a nigga."

"Are you kidding me right now? Our daughter is out there somewhere, and all you can talk to me about is how I left you. You ain't changed shit but your drawers since I been gone, nigga." I could feel the tears bubbling up and splashing onto my cheeks. "This was a bad idea. I'm going back to my mother's house. I can't do this."

Frenchie reached out to grab my wrists, but I snatched away. "Just hold up, Elite. Talk to me."

"I can't," I said, fighting back more tears.

"Please, Elite. Don't leave me. Not like this. I'm sorry for what I said, aight? You know I can't stand to see you cry."

"What you did... it's unforgivable. You put our family in

danger. Our child is missing because of you! This is beyond all the lies and the cheating. Half of my heart is out there missing... I—I can't. I just want to talk to my baby girl. I need to hear her voice, Frenchie. I need to hear her tell me she loves me. What if she's hurt or hungry or scared? What if she's crying? I need my baby back, Frenchie. Tell me you'll get our daughter back."

"I told you I'm gon' fix it, and I meant that shit, aight? I just need you here with me. I need you back, E. You my rib. A nigga can barely breathe without you."

"What we have... had, it isn't healthy. We're supposed to grow together, not apart."

"I'm not tryna be apart, Elite. It's hard, aight? It's hard fuckin' bein' without you." His nostrils flared.

I scoffed. "I bet it is hard, but it's your actions that made us this way, and with all this shit going on right now, Imani is the only thing I can think about. I never want to let Paxton out of my sight.

"Then let me be there for you, for our family," he said, swiping his hand across my stomach.

I quickly swatted his hand away. "Frenchie, don't."

"Why not?"

Tears shimmered in my eyes. "I-I lost the baby..." My words came undone as soon as I started, and my voice trailed off.

"W-what? Why didn't you tell me? You shouldn't have had to go through that alone."

"I'm a big girl. I can take care of myself."

He sighed with a defeated look on his face. "Are you okay?"

"No, but that wouldn't be the first time I was broken and still kept breathing," I told him.

"Why you always gotta act so tough? You can't stand here and tell me that you don't love me."

"You know I do. I always will, but you wanna know why being without me is hard? Because you just finally realized that I've been your security blanket this entire time. I have two kids with you, Frankie. I never thought I'd have to raise you, too."

I picked Paxton up from his swing and grabbed his diaper bag and my purse to leave. Frenchie leaned against the arm of the couch and watched me head to the door in silence. As soon as my hand gripped the knob, he spoke up.

"Just think about it, please. You're my world, Elite. You're my peace, Elite."

I shook my head at him before stepping outside into the cold air. "And you're my pain, Frenchie."

FRENCHIE

I woke up on the living room floor, alone. There was white residue on my hands and across my nose as if I'd been playing in pure flour all night long. I crawled to my feet and staggered into the downstairs bathroom. My glossy eyes caught my reflection in the mirror, and I shook my head is disgust. Elite being gone broke my heart into even smaller pieces. I needed to see her. Just her aura alone did something to me, put me in a better headspace. There was no doubt that my mind was drowning in darkness. I was spiraling, and I had to get my shit together before I lost all the shit I cared about. Elite's last words to me cut me deeper than any knife ever could. Peace no longer resided anywhere near me.

My feet pushed back into the living room, and I fell back against the couch with a thud. I closed my eyes. The house smelled like whiskey and marijuana. My eyes slowly cracked open and met an empty liquor bottle lying next to an ashtray with two half-smoked blunts in it. I was neglecting the fact that I needed to face my issues instead of self-medicating to escape my fucked up ass reality—the cocaine and liquor weren't enough to numb the pain of my past. Growing up, Pharaoh had always been the smart one. The good one, even. In comparison to me, he was an angel in Big Mama's eyes. Yeah, his mother left him at four, but at least he could hold on to the hope that she was still alive. My mother was dead, and she was never coming back.

I was never one to blame my father's actions on the way I turned out. I was his first born and having kids of my own. I understood if he didn't know what the fuck he was doing. I felt the same way at times. With shit around me already spiraling like it was, losing my daughter would send me off the deep end for good. I had to do what he couldn't do. I had to save myself before I could save Imani.

I grabbed one of the blunts from the ashtray and lit it to let my head get lost in a cloud of marijuana smoke. I sat in my filth and listened to the silence as memories flooded my head. I was all alone with no answers and a hell of a lot of questions. I guess Elite figured a nigga needed to know how it felt to be alone. I hated it. My phone vibrated face down against the carpet, and I groaned. I picked up the phone and answered it. "Hello?"

"9301 South Minson Street in two days, two o'clock in the morning."

A vein popped out of my neck. "Put her on the phone," I said through gritted teeth. All I smelled was alcohol and Kush on my breath when I spoke.

"Fuck you."

"Put her on the phone or else I ain't givin' you shit."

Sweat beaded my forehead as I held the phone to my ear longing to hear anything other than silence.

"D-daddy?" Imani said.

Just hearing her tiny voice sent a wave of shame washing over me. "It's me, baby girl. Everything is going to be okay. I'm coming to get you."

"Don't fuck this up, nigga," Xae said and hung up.

My hand shook with rage as I lowered the phone from my ear. Suddenly, my chest tightened, and I couldn't breathe. I felt like a fish out of water. A single tear slipped down my face, and I lost it. I catapulted the phone from one side of the room to the other and punched the air around me. I was choking on my anger so much that I punched three holes straight through the drywall, sending pieces of crumbled wall falling to the ground. I pulled my bloody fists back and wiped them off on my shirt. I went from shedding tears to going straight poker-faced like I was a crazy mothafucka. All that toxic shit in my system had my ass all the way up that I didn't even feel my knuckles begin to swell.

I ran down to my stash spot in the basement and picked up the duffel bag with what was left of the drugs and cash inside. Once I was back upstairs, I pushed all the unopened mail to the side on the dining room table and pulled everything out to see exactly how much I had. There were two bricks that were still untouched, and the seven-hundred and fifty thousand that I thought I had left of the full two.

I needed to talk to Elite to see if she would lend me money from the shop and then once we had our daughter back, I would spend however long making sure she got every cent back, plus interest. The phone rang four times before she answered.

"What do you want, Frenchie?"

"Look, I know I'm the last nigga you wanna talk to, but I need to see you."

"I'm not coming over there."

"I'll come to you."

"I don't want you here either."

"Look, it's important."

"If it's that important, you'd stop wasting time and just tell me now."

"Fine. I got the call with the time and the place to meet these niggas to get Imani back. P is helpin' me get the bricks and Riot put up some money. As much as I hate to ask you—"

"How much do you need?" she asked, cutting me off.

"If I can get some money from Pharaoh and see what strings I can pull on my end, then I still might be anywhere from five-hundred thousand to seven-hundred and fifty thousand dollars short, and I was hoping I could get it from you from the shop, you know, as a loan."

"I'm not givin' you money from my shop, Frenchie."

"Fuck you mean? It was my money that helped build that shit up anyway." The line went silent for a few seconds. "H-hello?"

"I'm here."

I sighed. "Look, the bottom line is, if I don't get the money in the next couple of days, then—"

She raised her voice to cut me off. "Don't say it!"

"I know I made my bed, and I gotta lay in that shit. I get that. This is me trying to make shit right. I just need you to help me do this."

"I'll be over in an hour," she told me and hung up.

I left everything on the table and walked upstairs to the bathroom while pulling the bloodstained shirt over my head and tossing it to the floor. I leaned in to turn on the shower and then hovered over the sink while I waited for the water to get piping hot. My eyes landed on their reflection in the mirror once more, and all I could do was shake my head. *You gotta get your shit together, nigga,* I thought to myself.

I pulled all my clothes off and stepped inside the shower, letting the water slice over my back. I splashed the hot water on my face, letting my beard get soakin' wet. The open wounds on my fists stung underneath the water as I lathered up my washcloth with soap, being sure to wash every ounce of drugs or alcohol out of my system. I ran my hands down my chest, then ducked my entire head underneath the showerhead. Dark thoughts danced through my head like sugarplum fairies. I had to figure out a way to get the money fast. I was going to get my daughter back by any means necessary. One thing was for sure, time wasn't on my side.

BY THE TIME Elite got to the house, I was standing in the dining room with no shirt on, still contemplating what the fuck I was going to do to get what I needed.

"Hurry up and close the door. It's cold outside," I told her.

"No one told you to be in here with no shirt on like it's ninety degrees outside," she said while turning up her nose as she closed the door behind her. With her hand resting on her hip, she picked up the empty liquor bottle lying by her foot and looked at me. "You takin' shots for breakfast now?"

I shrugged. "The breakfast of champions."

"Yeah, well I hope you found what you were looking for in the bottom of that bottle," she scoffed.

Her eyes landed on the gaping holes in the wall. Without saying anything, she turned to look at me with a look on her face that told me if she opened her mouth, I wouldn't like what would come out.

"I'll get it fixed," I told her. All she did was shake her head at me. "How are you?" I asked in an attempt to change the subject.

"How do you think I am?" she snapped back.

"Where's Pax?"

"He's fine. He's with my mother."

"Why didn't you bring him?" I asked.

Without responding, she turned her attention to the drugs and money spread out on the table while rocking back and forth on the balls of her feet.

"So this is what you stole?"

"What's left of it."

"You just had all these fuckin' pounds sittin' right up under my nose this entire time?" She was fuming.

"It was better that you didn't know."

"Bullshit!"

My eyes tore over her uncomfortable demeanor. Although her lips were saying shit, I could read her body language well. There was something she wanted to get off her chest but was letting her pride hold her back.

"Why you don't look me in the eyes anymore when you talk to me, Elite?"

"I don't know what you're talking about," she said, casting her gaze onto the lamp by the couch.

"There it is right there. Look at me when I'm talkin' to you. You want to teach me a lesson? Fine. You did that shit, aight? But if you got somethin' you wanna say to me, then say that shit right the fuck now, Elite."

"If I had somethin' to say, I'd say it."

"Then stop lyin' and tell me the truth," I told her.

"You want the truth? Fine. The truth is, it's hard for me to even look at you, Frenchie. When I look at you, all I see is Imani, and then I'm reminded of how much I hate you."

Her words struck me like a bolt of lightning. "I'm sorry for everything, aight? I want my family back as much as you do."

She shook her head. "Here," she said, pulling a folded piece of paper out of her back pocket and handing it to me.

"What is this?"

"It's the number to the safety deposit box at the bank where we set up the rainy-day account in Imani's name."

"You've still been puttin' money into it?"

"I never stopped. You have access to it. Take out what you need and go get our daughter."

"Don't worry. I'm gon' bring our baby girl back home. I promise."

Chapter Eight

PHARAOH

"Hello?" I answered the phone for Riot after placing my to-go order at the soul food spot.

"Yo, I got some good news."

"What is it?"

"I got word about the whereabouts of that nigga Xae. I heard him and some of his niggas be over at that new club that just opened up a couple weeks ago."

"You tell French?"

"Nah, not yet."

"Good, don't. The nigga ain't got it all together right now. I don't want him to see the nigga and do somethin' crazy."

"Bet."

"How'd you find out about this?"

"Girl I been fuckin' with works there. She said they always buyin' out the bar, blowin' cash and shit."

"You sure it's them?"

"Only way to find out is to go see for ourselves, but she said the nigga with the money name is Xae."

"Aight. Well let's go see about it later tonight then. I'll swing by your crib around eleven."

I hung up and watched the waitress as she made her way across the room to bring me my food. She had a petite frame and a honey golden skin complexion. Her hair was dyed a mix of burgundy and orange.

"I know you." She smiled, flashing her white teeth at me.

"Nah, I don't think you do."

"No, I didn't mean it like that. I meant, I know you as in

I've seen you here a few times before."

"Yeah, I come here sometimes."

"The last time I saw you here, you were with a girl."

"Yo, you nosy."

"I'd prefer to use the term observant." She giggled, then handed my food to me.

"Thank you."

"No problem. I'll see you around."

I turned to walk out of the restaurant and crossed the street back to my car when I heard someone call out my name. My neck jerked in the direction, and I locked eyes with Savannah. She let a few cars drive past before making her way over to me.

"Hey," she said. Instead of responding, I looked at her with a blank stare. "Please say something, Pharaoh. Don't just leave me standing here feeling crazier than I already do."

"I would've thought you'd been halfway back to wherever the fuck you came from by now."

She pressed her lips in a hard line. "Any word on Imani?" she asked, changing the subject.

"That's none of your business."

A sigh escaped her lips as she lowered her gaze down to the ground. My hand tightened around the to-go bag of food. "It's too cold to just be standin' outside shootin' the shit, aight? And if my food get cold, I'm gon' be mad as fuck."

"Do you think you'll ever stop hating me?" she asked.

I shifted my weight from one foot to the other, then looked into her eyes for the first time. "I don't hate you, Savannah."

"That's probably the nicest thing you've said to me since…"

"Since what? Since you got me arrested?"

"Can we just start over as people? Not Pharaoh the infamous drug dealer or Savannah the undercover FBI agent. We're so much more than just titles, Pharaoh. I know you know that."

"Nah, I'm good."

"If it means anything to you, I quit. I'm just another regular girl standing here, looking for a fresh start with you."

It would've been easy for me to tell her how bad she'd fucked my head up, or even how much I still thought about her, craved her. My pride would never make it that easy on her.

"Do you have plans tonight?"

"Yeah, I do," I told her. "I'm going to check out this club that just opened up not too long ago. Heard the nigga that took Frenchie's daughter hangs around there."

"So you do know who took her. Why didn't you tell me? I want to help."

"There ain't shit you can do, aight? Just leave it alone."

"Can you just promise me that you won't do anything stupid?"

I couldn't answer her question, at least not the way I knew she wanted me to. I was going to meet with the nigga on Frenchie's behalf to see if we could come to a common ground long enough for Imani to be returned safe and sound, and then all bets were off.

RIOT AND I pulled up to the club, and there was a line of people waiting outside to be let in. Mostly groups of females with short ass dresses and four-inch heels. We walked straight up to the bouncer, and he let us in. Colored lights flashed throughout the establishment as Riot and I pushed through the hot stuffy air of the crowd. A girl stepped on my shoe with her heel and I frowned. "Yo, watch out."

"I am so sorry," she said, looking up at me.

I looked down at her and realized she was the waitress from the restaurant earlier. I'd gone from never noticing her at all to seeing her twice in the same day. The last time she said she'd seen me, I was too wrapped up in Savannah to notice anyone else.

"Funny running into you twice in one day," she told me.

"Must be your lucky day," I joked while looking her up and down. She had on a tight red dress that exposed her cleavage and her toned thighs.

"Must be."

"I never did get your name."

"Shayla."

"Pharaoh."

"What brings you out tonight?"

"I'm here for my sister's bachelorette party. She's the one with the white dress, sash, and drunk as hell."

"Damn, she's fucked up."

"Tell me about it, and the wedding is tomorrow, believe it or not."

"Damn."

"At least she's having a good time."

"Word. Well, I'll let you get back to her."

"Maybe I'll save you a dance before the night is over."

I nodded. "Aight."

For the rest of the night, I watched Shayla from across the room fanning herself after each twerk session with her girls and turning every nigga down that came her way looking for a dance. I pulled out my phone to check the time and saw an unread text message from Savannah. My eyes rolled as the waitress walked over to our section with a glowing tray topped with sparkling bottles of Hennessy and Cîroc.

"Are you sure that nigga is gon' be here?" I asked Riot while he poured himself another drink. "It's already one o'clock in the morning."

"Yeah, I'm sure. I got it on good authority that this is where he and a few niggas in his crew come every Friday night."

"Niggas better hurry up. I'm really not tryna be here much longer."

"Chill out, nigga, and grab a shot."

"Nah, I need a clear head just in case I gotta break a nigga's jaw in here tonight."

"Suit yourself." He shrugged.

Against everything in me, I pulled my phone out of my pocket again and read Savannah's message.

Savannah: It was good seeing you today. I miss you.

I rolled my eyes and shoved my phone back in my pocket. I looked over in Shayla's section again and watched her and her squad take their talents to the dance floor, and all eyes were on them. My feet stood planted firmly on the ground while I baby-sat a cup of liquor I knew I wasn't going to drink. Shayla twerked with her friends, while laughing and having what looked like the time of her life.

"See something you like?" Riot yelled at me over the music.

I shrugged. "Nah."

"Stop lyin', nigga. I saw you talkin' to her earlier. Who is she?"

"Just some girl I met at the restaurant."

"Yo, I know you tryna be the bigger man and all that other shit, but why don't you try letting loose and being a dog for once, nigga? She not lookin' over here for no reason."

I shook my head then set the cup down on the table. He was right. I didn't know why a part of me was still holding onto Savannah as if we could ever be anything more than two people on the opposite sides of the law. The DJ changed the song, and the crowd went wild. I watched Shayla scan the club until her eyes locked on mine. She walked over to my section and waved for me to come over to her. I shook my head, and she made her way right up to me.

"What, you don't dance or somethin'?"

"Nah," I told her.

"Well you're going to dance tonight. I'm not taking no for an answer," she said as she turned around and pressed her body against mine.

I held her petite waist as she backed her ass up against my dick, popping it to the bass. As good of a dancer as she was, my mind was all over the place. One second, I was wrapped up in trying to find that nigga Xae, and the next I was trying to push thoughts of Savannah out of my head.

Riot tapped my shoulder. "You see them niggas over there

that just walked in? That's gotta be them."

I directed my attention over to their section and watched them throw up their gang signs, take bottles of liquor to the head and flood their section with a bunch of females. Out of all of them, one in particular stood out. He had more ice on him than a glacier and was sending the waitresses back and forth to the bar to bring back new bottles of Ace of Spades.

"Yeah, there he go right there," I told Riot.

"What you wanna do?"

I looked down at Shayla, who was still wrapped up in the bass of the music. "I'll be back, I whispered in her ear."

The smell of sweat hung in the air as Riot and I made our way over to their section. As soon as I went to take the first step up, one of his niggas held his arm out to block me. I looked down at his hand and then looked up at his face. "Yo, chill," I told him. "I just wanna speak to your boy."

"Nah, not tonight."

"It's about business, no bullshit."

"It's cool, let 'em through," Xae said, waving his hand for us to come over to him.

Once my path to him was clear, I walked up to him with Riot standing a foot behind me. He held out his hand to dap me up. "I'm Xae."

"I know who you are. I'm Pharaoh."

"I know who you are, too."

"Good, so now that we got all the bullshit out the way, let's talk business."

"I don't have any business wit you, Pharaoh."

"Yeah, I think you do."

He let out an effortless chuckle before tossing back whatever was left in his cup. "I ain't gon' lie to you. You got some balls comin' up to me when I'm tryna unwind with my niggas, when one call from me could mean the difference between his daughter having another birthday party or a funeral."

My jaw clenched. "I'm sure there's a way to handle this where we can all be happy, and it doesn't have to end in blood."

He scoffed while widening his stance. "Your fuckin' cousin was reckless and tried to kill my fuckin' brother over there." He pointed to a younger lookin' nigga with dark skin, and I took a mental photo of his face. "Niggas wanna rob me and think I'm not gon' find out and bring the heat right to your fuckin' front door, nigga. I don't tolerate disrespect from fuckin' nobody, aight?"

"That shit goes both ways," I reminded him.

"I made that shit back the next night, but that's not the fuckin' point. You a businessman, right? Well, so am I. I bet you fifty bands right now if you were me, you would've done the same thing."

"Nah, the difference between you and me is I would've never sat around playin' around on the phone. I would've found you, walked right up to you, and started bussin'."

"Is that right?" he asked, reaching for his waist.

"Yeah, that's right. That's how I play the game." My eyes darted around and landed on the half empty liquor bottle an inch away from my hand.

"Well I ain't never gon' play by the rules of your game. Your family fucked with mine, so I'm fuckin' with his right back. I ain't got no beef with you, Pharaoh, but if you wanna take it there, I ain't got no problem doin' that."

As tired as I was of having the pissing contest with him, I knew Riot and I were outnumbered. We were in MCF territory, but I still didn't give a fuck. I was going to have to show him who the real boss in Chicago was. There was enough money to go around so that everyone could eat and live their lives how they wanted to, but he wasn't going to be doing it in my city for much longer.

"Why don't you just calm down before shit goes left in this mothafucka," I said, leaning into him.

He took a few steps back and scowled at me. "One call and I'll slit her little ass throat. I told that nigga what I want, and I told him when to bring that shit to me. Ain't shit else up for discussion, nigga. Now why don't you just go back over to your section before shit gets hectic!"

A few of his boys snickered while he lifted up his shirt to show off his gun. I'd never backed down before, and I wasn't about to start for a nigga who I knew was pussy. I quickly grabbed the bottle, broke it against the table and held it to his throat. "I'll spill your blood all over this fuckin' club, nigga. Don't you ever in your life fuckin' disrespect me like that again," I warned him.

Within seconds, all hell broke loose. Guns were drawn, and people were screaming as security rushed the entire section. It took five security guards to shove both Riot and I outside, and we made our way over to the car just before they started to evacuate everyone out of the club. I unlocked the car door and grabbed my gun from underneath the seat. I was posted up on the side of my car, waiting. Fuming.

"I swear to God I wanna kill that mothafucka!" I yelled, while cocking my gun.

"He gon' get his day, believe that," Riot added.

"Where the fuck that nigga get off talkin' to me like he tough? Keep talkin' that shit, I got somethin' for his ass. Call up the soldiers."

Riot pulled out his phone and started making phone calls. My blood was boiling as I rested my finger on the trigger. Normally, it would take a lot for any nigga to pull me out of my character, but that nigga had done it instantly, and I wasn't afraid to end his life. With my gun resting against my lap, I watched everyone flood out of the doors of the club. Out of the sea of people standing around, smoking, spitting game or waiting for their rides, I saw Savannah. She was standing off to the side, applying some lip gloss like the club wasn't being evacuated. After staring a little too long in her direction, I put my gun in the back of my pants.

"Yo, I'll be back," I told Riot.

"Where the fuck you goin', nigga?"

"I said I'll be back, just stay here."

The second I was in arms reach of her, I grabbed her arm.

"What the fuck are you doing here?" I scolded her.

"Maybe I came to have a drink."

"I don't give a fuck why you came. You need to go home. Now, Savannah. I'm not fuckin' playin' with you tonight, aight? I'm already on a thousand, and I don't need you getting in the way of shit."

Before she could respond, Shayla walked up beside me and looped her arm in mine. "There you are. I thought you told me you'd be right back. I've been looking all over for you."

I shot my eyes over at her and then looked back at Savannah. She was never good at hiding what she felt. It would always show up right on her face. "Who is this?" She frowned.

"I'm Shayla... and you're... wait, I'm a lil' drunk right now... the girl from the restaurant, right?"

"Excuse me?"

"I work at the soul food spot you two came to once."

The frown never left Savannah's face as she sized her up. "Am I missing something here?" she asked me.

"Nah."

Shayla was too drunk to realize she was probably in danger for walking up to me in front of Savannah, but a part of me wanted to see how far things would go. Shayla turned her attention to me and rested her hand on my chest. "I was wondering if you could help me take my sister to our Uber over there. She's nothing but dead weight in heels right now, and I don't want us to miss our ride."

"Uh, yeah, sure."

"Thank you so much."

The two of us left Savannah standing there, and I knew she was in her feelings. I helped Shayla get her sister into the back seat of the Uber. "Thank you again."

"No problem."

"You know what I've been wondering all night?"

"What?"

"Why you haven't asked me for my number yet." She smiled.

I pressed my lips together. "Maybe some other time. Get home safe, aight?"

As soon as the door to Shayla's Uber shut, gunshots rang out. I instinctively ducked down while pulling my gun out of my pants. My eyes searched the area for Savannah, and once I saw her, I instinctively ran to her and shielded her body with my own. After the gun fire ceased, I looked down at her.

"Are you okay?"

"I-I think so."

I looked down at her dress and saw blood on it. "There's blood on you."

She looked down at her body and then looked at me. "Pharaoh, that's not my blood."

SAVANNAH

My heart stopped.

My fingertips went numb.

All I saw was Pharaoh's blood spilling out onto the cold pavement, and I was terrified. "Oh my God, Pharaoh, no!" I screamed.

One second my body was crushed underneath the weight of him, the next Pharaoh was laying in my arms gasping for air. His body had gone into shock, and pools of his blood started bubbling up and falling out the corners of his mouth.

"Yo, what the fuck!" Riot yelled, running over to us with a

frantic look across his face.

I locked my hand underneath his head. "Look at me, Pharaoh. Look at me, baby. It's going to be okay." I pulled out my phone to call 9-1-1, when Riot yelled.

"Help me get him in the car. We don't have time to wait for a fuckin' ambulance!"

"If we move him now, he'll bleed out. We can't move him until I can try and stop the bleeding."

All I could hear were dozens of high heels clicking quickly across the pavement, scattering to safety as I ripped a piece of fabric off my dress and pressed it into his chest wound to try and stop his blood from pouring out like a faucet.

"Just hold on, nigga. It's gon' be aight," Riot told him as he kneeled down beside me and held his hand.

AS SOON AS we got to the hospital, the paramedics rushed out to the car and took Pharaoh into emergency surgery to remove the bullet that was wedged in his chest cavity. Once the stretcher was behind the double doors, I turned my attention to Riot who had slid his back against the bleached white hospital wall.

"I can't lose my nigga, yo," he said, burying his head in his hands.

"You won't. They are going to do everything they can to save him."

He shook his head as if he didn't believe me. "You don't get it. Fuckin' prison visitation rooms or fuckin' funeral homes. That's all my niggas ever fuckin' see."

"You can't think like that."

"I'll think however the fuck I want. Don't act like I don't know what you did to my nigga, aight? You may have done your part in helpin' to keep him alive, but you still a fuckin' Fed," he growled.

I lowered my head. He'd already had his mind made up about me, and I didn't blame him. His opinion didn't matter to me. The only person's opinion I cared about was Pharaoh's, and if he didn't make it off the operating table, then none of it would even matter. My feet shuffled down the hallway, and soon, Riot got up to follow. He pulled his phone out of his pocket and walked outside to brave the chilling Chicago night air. I watched him through the window in the emergency room waiting room as he paced back and forth. After about ten minutes, he came back in and walked over to me.

"Any word yet?"

"They haven't been back there that long," I told him.

"Fuck, man! As much as I don't wanna leave, I gotta go figure out how the fuck we gon' get them niggas back ASAP," he huffed.

"Go do whatever it is you gotta do. I'll be here. I'm not going anywhere."

"It shouldn't be you he sees when he comes out of surgery."

I chewed the inside of my lip, trying hard not to cuss his ass out. We were both riding high off our emotions, and I didn't want to make the night go any worse than it already had. "Like I said, I'm not going anywhere," I repeated.

He clenched his jaw and then took a few steps back toward the door. "Tell my nigga I'll be back."

I nodded, and he turned to leave. My hands sat clasped in my lap as my heels clicked against the waiting room floor. An hour and a half passed before someone came out to speak to me. "How is he?" I asked the doctor.

"He's stable, but he did lose a lot of blood. We're in the process of giving him a blood transfusion now."

"Is he awake? Can I please see him?"

"It may be best that you come back in the morning. I just wanted to give you an update."

"Please, I—I just need to see with my own eyes that he's okay," I pleaded.

He pressed his lips into a hard line and then nodded. "Follow me down the hall. I'll take you up to his room."

"Thank you so much."

"If anybody should be giving thanks here, it should be him. If it wasn't for you trying to clot his blood with your dress, he probably wouldn't have made it."

"Wait, how'd you know that I—"

He pointed down to the uneven hem in my dress from where I tore some fabric off, and I nodded. "Good work," he told me.

AFTER HOURS OF sitting in the worn-out visitor's chair, watching Pharaoh's chest rise and fall over and over again while listening to the sound of his LED heart monitor beeping, the nurse had been kind enough to bring me an extra pillow to make it a little more comfortable. He lay shirtless with an IV stuck in his right arm and dozens of wires leading to machines to monitor every vital in his body, and a large piece of dressing on his chest to cover where the bullet had pierced his back and landed in his chest.

I woke up to Pharaoh staring a hole in the side of my face. After rubbing my eyes, I spoke up. "You're awake."

"You been here all night?"

"What time is it?" I asked, stretching my limbs.

He looked over at the clock on the wall, then back at me. "Almost seven thirty."

"Yeah, I guess I have. How are you feeling?"

"Like I got a hole in my fuckin' chest."

I shook my head. "I thought I told you not to do anything stupid."

He shrugged lazily. "Guess I didn't listen. You should already know I'll do whatever it takes to protect my family."

"I know, but look where it got you."

"I don't even know how the fuck I got here."

"Riot drove you while I kept trying to slow down the bleeding, so the good news is, you're alive. Bad news is, your back seats are probably ruined."

I watched him crush the hospital sheets with his fingertips and then tilt his head back against the pillow. "That's why your dress is ripped?" he asked with his eyes closed.

I nodded. "Yeah."

"You should go home and change out of that shit."

"I just needed to make sure you were okay."

"I'm straight. Breathin' a lil' funny, but I'm good."

"Yeah, the doctors said you would be breathing differently for a while."

"What else did they tell you?"

"That you probably wouldn't have made it if it wasn't for me."

"Bullshit."

"I'm not lying to you. You can ask Riot!"

"Where is he? Is he okay?"

"He's fine. He went to go tell everyone what happened. I told him I'd stay with you and let you know that he really wasn't trying to leave. He'll probably be back within a few hours."

I watched him nod as he opened and closed his eyes. "Are you okay?"

"Tired."

"You just need to rest now."

"Yeah."

"Before I go, I just have one question."

"What?"

"What made you come back for me?"

"The only reason I was there in the first place was to try and clean up the mess French made. You never should've fuckin' been there in the first place. It could've been you sittin' in this mothafucka instead of me."

"I know. Thank you for keeping me safe. I owe you everything, Pharaoh. You saved my life."

"From what you told me, you saved mine, too, so we even."

I nodded without verbally saying a word and turned to leave.

"Yo, Savannah, wait a second."

I turned back to him. "Yeah?"

"This is probably the pain medication talking, but whatever you did to keep me alive, thank you."

I cracked a soft smile as I walked over and rested my hand on the side railing of his bed. "I don't know what I would've done if you weren't here," I said, swiping my hand across the side of his face.

He turned his head away from me, and I turned it back to gently kiss his lips. "I love you, Pharaoh, and I'm glad you're okay."

I walked out of the room and thanked my lucky stars all the way to the car that Pharaoh was okay. I'd seen him face down death and win. As soon as the Uber pulled out of the fire zone, my phone rang. "Hello?"

"Hey, any update?"

"Yes and no," I said, followed by a yawn.

"You sound tired."

"I am. Pharaoh got shot last night. I'm just now leaving the hospital."

"Well, you're not crying so that must mean he's still alive."

"He is. Have you heard from Elite since you've been out of the hospital?"

"Yeah. I'm meeting with her in a few hours."

"Good for you. I hope everything works out the way you want it to."

"Thanks. I mean, a part of me knows that she may never forgive me, but I'm not gon' give up until she tells me to."

If anyone knew that forgiveness was a hard pill to swallow, it was me. All I could do was continue to be there for Pharaoh in any way I could. I'd never chased after a man the way I'd chased after him. I loved every square inch of his being, and I would fight until I couldn't swing anymore.

ELITE

I loved the smell of coffee. The entire coffeehouse smelled like aromatic coffee blends and caramel as soon as I walked in. I rested my elbows on the long counter in front of me. Behind the barista were a row of chrome expresso machines. Once I got my drink, I scooted into a booth toward the back of the establishment and waited.

I turned the cup up to my lips. "Ah, shit!" I winced from the scalding coffee burning my tongue.

"Too hot for you?"

I looked up and saw Michael walking over to me. "I don't even know why I tried. I knew it was hot," I said while shaking my head.

He took his seat and blew on his hot drink while gripping the warm mug in his hands. "I'll be sure to be careful."

I smiled. "Good."

"So… you wanted to talk…"

"Talk, yes. Thank you for coming."

"Thank you for calling," he said. "There was a time when I didn't think you ever would."

"To be honest, I hadn't planned on it."

"What changed your mind?"

"I-um, I had a miscarriage."

My eyes shot down to my cup and then slowly made their way across the table to him. I watched him shift his posture in the seat and then clear his throat. "I thought you were getting an abortion..."

"I know. I never got the chance to. After my daughter got kidnapped, it was like my mind was paralyzed, and I couldn't think about anything else. I still can't."

He lowered his eyes down to the chai tea that was sitting in front of him. "When did this happen?"

"A few days ago. One minute I was at work, and everything was fine, then out of nowhere, I got this sharp cramping feeling in my stomach, so I went to the bathroom and saw that I was bleeding. I went to the hospital and they confirmed it. It's over, Michael."

"A few days ago? And I'm just hearing from you about this?"

"I know, and I'm sorry, I just—"

"Fuck all that. You should've told me sooner so that I could've been there for you, Elite."

"How would you have been there for me? Listen to yourself. Do you seriously still have this fictional relationship between us going anywhere other than where it is right now? Stop it!"

"How fictional is it? You know everything about me now. We can start over. The baby doesn't change how I feel about you."

I shook my head. He wasn't getting it. I was the only one living in the present out of the two of us, and there were probably a million reasons why we couldn't have the relationship that both of us wanted. "This is for the best. How would I have explained it to Frenchie? To anyone? He thought the baby was his, and now that there is no more baby, I'm not saying anything to him, and now that you know, we can really just call this closure and go back to whatever is left of our lives. You go back to doing your job, and I'll go back to trying to bring my daughter back home where she belongs."

"How is the search for her going?"

"I didn't even know you knew she was missing..."

"Yeah, Savannah told me."

I sighed. "I don't know. Frenchie said he's working on it, that he's got it handled, and that he's going to bring her back home."

"Do you believe him?" he asked.

"I don't know what I believe anymore."

"Are you over him?" he asked.

"What?"

"You heard me... It's the second time you've brought him up since I sat down. It's okay if you aren't; just be honest with me."

I pursed my lips together and cast my gaze down to my fiddling thumbs. "I love him, and yet, I still don't have any feelings for him at all. Frenchie makes me numb to everything; the love, the hate... they're both there. I just can't tell the difference between them."

"You know that with all the shit I know, I could have him locked up for a long time. The only reason I would even consider dropping everything I have against French is because of you. If he's who you want to be with... I don't want you or your kids spending the next twenty years looking at him through a jail cell."

I nodded slowly, unsure of what to say back to him.

"You got this crazy ass wall built up—"

"I know," I said, cutting him off.

"And I'm tellin' you that you need to make room in your heart to love the right nigga, Elite. I can't make you fall in love with me. I can't make you do anything you don't want to do, but stop paralyzing yourself with the thought that you don't

103

deserve better than what the fuck you've been gettin' all these years."

I sat there, drumming my fingers against the coffee cup with my expression dulled. "Trust me, this is what's best. Get out while you can, Michael. I'm damaged goods. I have more baggage than your average woman. I trigger easily. You said it yourself, I have the Great Wall of China around my heart."

"And if you would've let me finish, you would've heard me tell you that I was fully prepared to love you and your scars while climbing to the top of that shit. You're so used to being loved wrong that even the possibility of being loved the right way scares you."

My face twisted as I tried to hold back tears. "I just want to feel alive again, and you... you made me feel that... but I can't, Michael."

"Don't let Frenchie be the reason why you not eating or sleeping. You need to take care of yourself, Elite. If you no good to you, you no good to anybody."

Whether he knew it or not, I was saving his life. If anyone found out that the baby I lost wasn't Frenchie's, he wouldn't stop until he killed both Michael and I, and it didn't matter if he was a Fed or not. Building a life with me meant constantly looking over his shoulder, bending the rules, and breaking the law.

"When are you going to be real with yourself and admit that you're stuck in a sea of your own insecurities? Even the nigga you was with wasn't brave enough to cross that shit. You know why? Because he helped you fill that sea, Elite. I was the nigga that was brave enough to swim out and save you, and I'm here right now for you, Elite. Why the fuck can't you see that?"

"I do see that, and that's the problem! I can't give you what you can give me!"

"Just don't tell me you never felt anything for me. I remember the way your eyes sparkled when I kissed you for the first time. Don't make me out to be crazy," he said, outstretching his hand to grab mine.

I quickly pulled my hand away and looked at him in silence. The longer he sat in front of me, I could feel my heart shattering over and over like a broken record.

"I guess no response is a response in itself." He shrugged. "So this is it, huh?"

I nodded. "Yeah, it is."

He sighed. "Is this really what you want? Because if it is, I'll get up right now, and I'll be on a flight back to Atlanta by the morning. But if there is the tiniest part of you that wants me to stay, to fight, tell me now."

As much as I wanted to close my eyes and wake up in a world where it was just my kids, Michael and I, I knew better. I watched him get up and hover over the table. "Goodbye, Elite," he whispered in my ear then kissed my cheek.

I held my breath until I could no longer see him walking away. I was stone cold crazy for letting the best man I'd ever known slip right through my fingers. If you loved someone, you had to let them go, and that's what I'd done for him. No matter what his name was or his occupation, Michael was a great man. He was built with good character, determination, and a warmth inside his heart that encapsulated every part of mine. I was woman enough to know that I was no match for him, and instead of dragging him through the mud like Frenchie had done me, I was strong enough to let him be free.

Chapter Nine

PHARAOH

The moment I took a bullet for Savannah, I knew that she was going to be the fuckin' death of me. I was still laid up in my hospital bed on pain meds that had me feelin' like I was moon walkin'. As loopy in the head as I might've been, I still had Savannah's ass on my mind. Knowing that she had a hand in making sure I stayed alive made me feel a way. Resisting her became less and less of an option. No matter how many times I told myself I didn't give a fuck, I'd gotten wrapped up into her too fast, and she'd become my kryptonite.

There was a knock on the door that pulled me out of my thoughts. I watched my lawyer walk in. He had on a cashmere heather gray suit, crisp white collared shirt, and a burgundy tie. Even over top of the hospital smell, I knew he smelled like money.

"I must be paying you well," I told him.

"Very well."

"You got good news for me?"

"I do."

"What's the verdict?" I asked.

"After doing some real digging into what the prosecution was trying to throw at you, I was able to go to the judge and get everything dismissed."

"Everything? Even all that shit from that Fed?"

"Yeah, he wouldn't go on record to say anything against you that would incriminate you or anyone he'd been around."

"For real?"

"Yes, he didn't leave a statement, so without him, they

can't prove that you were ever in possession of any of the drugs, nor have any relation with them at all. They did find drugs at the storage unit, but you were nowhere near it at the time, and it was not in your name, so there's no nexus between you or those drugs either. After all that, their side failed to provide substantial evidence."

"So it's all gone?"

He nodded. "All gone within the next twenty-four hours."

"Make sure you chew that shit up and spit it out!"

"I will be sure to do just that."

"Thank you."

"You're welcome, Pharaoh."

With all the charges dropped against me, I could finally start to breathe easy again. I'd avoided indictments since I'd been in the game, and I could only pray it continued until I was ready to hang it all up. As soon as he closed the door behind him, my phone rang. I looked at the screen and answered it. "What up, French?"

"Yo, you got the bricks for me?"

"Yeah, I got you. I already talked to Riot about it. He can get 'em to you."

"Aight, bet."

"You good?" I asked.

"I should be the one askin' you that, nigga. What the fuck was you thinkin' goin' out there to talk to that nigga because of me?"

"I was thinkin' you family, and that's what family do—look out for each other. You did it with me a thousand times."

He sighed, and I immediately could hear the uncertainty in his voice. "What's wrong?"

"Huh?"

"You heard me, nigga. Stop bullshittin' me."

"You remember when you told me you'd get me however much money I needed?"

"Yeah. How much?"

"I'm seven-hundred and fifty thousand short."

"Goddamn, French."

"I know, and that's with the money I had left, plus the shit from Riot, and I drained the rainy-day fund Elite had set up, and I'm still fuckin' short."

"You couldn't find no other faucet to tap?"

"Everything I thought I could get at fell through."

I sighed as I rubbed my chest. "You know I got you. When you need it by?"

"I need it right now, nigga. I'm meetin' with that mothafucka later tonight."

"What the fuck? When did y'all set that up? Why didn't you tell me?"

"This is some shit I gotta do on my own," he told me.

"Fuck that! You family. You not goin' alone."

"Nigga, you in a fuckin' hospital bed. Trust me, you've done enough. I'm gon' take it from here."

I stopped responding, knowing that French's mind was already made up. All I could do was pray he made it out alive in the end. "I'll make sure you have everything you need by tonight, even if I gotta bring it to you myself."

"Thank you."

"I love you, fam."

"Love you, too, fam," he said and ended the call.

FRENCHIE

My eyes opened in the middle of the night. Although I was still half asleep, I rolled over and wrapped my arms around the pillow on Elite's side of the bed, pulling it closer to my chest. After a few seconds of lying there with my eyes closed, I got up and got dressed to leave. I went to the closet and pulled out a small back duffel bag and threw it on top of the bed. I put on my rust colored Timbs, put my gun in the back of my jeans, and walked out of the house.

The cold wind howled like a pack of wolves as I headed to the car and threw the duffel bag in the back seat. The engine purred as I pulled the car into the street and headed to see Elite before doing a trade-off with Xae. I knocked on her mother's front door until she answered with her robe wrapped tightly around her body. "Frances, what are you doing here this late?" she asked, half asleep.

"I need to see Elite and Paxton."

"They are asleep."

"Please."

She stared me down for a few seconds, before taking a step to the side so I could come in. I walked down the hallway and opened the door to Elite's bedroom.

"Wake up, Elite," I whispered in her ear.

"Huh?"

"Listen to me."

"What's going on, Frenchie? What are you doing here?" she asked groggily.

"Shh. Stop talking and just listen. If I'm not back with Imani within the hour, leave with this bag and nothing else. Shoot anyone who comes through that door," I said, putting my gun in her hand.

"Frenchie, what are you about to do?" she asked with a hint of terror in her voice.

"Tell my son I love him," I said, bending down to kiss her forehead.

I disappeared into the blackness of the night and headed back to the car to go right my wrongs. The lust for blood pumped heavily through my veins. I was ready to set Terror Town on fire. I pulled up with both hands on the steering wheel. Xae hadn't requested for me to meet him just anywhere. He wanted me to meet him in the trap.

A part of me felt like I should've said a prayer before I got out, but I shook that shit off and reached underneath my seat to pull out my pistol, then got out to pop the trunk. I pulled out the bookbag with everything in it, tossed it over my shoulder, and closed the trunk. My boots shuffled against the concrete street as I walked up to the house that cast a shadow against the city street. I saw the cold air seeping through the bullet holes through the front windows from shootouts past.

After stepping on a cockroach with a twitching antenna, my foot stepped over the threshold, and the floors squeaked with every step thereafter. Inside, I noticed all the imperfections the old house possessed, from the walls laced with cobwebs up to the sections of the ceiling that hung low. The house cradled memories of crackheads enjoying their last high before overdosing. I slowly walked toward the back of the house where a single light was on. With my gun drawn, I swung around the corner and saw Bria standing inside. My forehead creased as I aimed my gun at her.

"Where the fuck is my daughter, Bria?"

"Did you bring what Xae asked for?"

"I said where the fuck is my daughter at!" I yelled.

As cold as it was inside the house, I was sweating bullets. She rolled her eyes at me. "She's in the other room, asleep. Where's the shit at?"

"Go get her, and I'll give it to you."

"That's not how this is going to work," Xae said, coming from out the corner of my eye.

I quickly turned to aim the gun in his direction and saw he already had one pointing at me. "Put it down, nigga, and do what the fuck I say. You're playing my game now, bitch nigga!" he yelled.

My body shook with rage as I snarled at him. My arms lowered slowly and then he lowered his. "All I want is my fuckin' daughter, nigga," I said, sounding more defeated than I should've.

"And if everything you owe me is with you, then that's what you'll get."

"It's all here," I told him, tossing the bag to the ground.

Bria walked over, retrieved the bag, and then walked back over to Xae. We both watched her unzip the bag and look inside. She pulled out all the kilos and the stacks of money. "It's all there," she said.

"Now go get my fuckin' daughter!" I yelled.

"Not quite. I want to talk to you first," Xae interrupted.

I could feel my patience wearing off by the second, and the bloodlust grew stronger inside of me. I was going to murder them both.

"About what, nigga? You mad I fucked your bitch or somethin'?"

"Nigga, fuck you!"

"Shut the fuck up, bitch." I snarled at her. "We good now, right? You got what you wanted. Now bring me my fuckin' daughter!"

"Yeah, I got what I wanted, but what makes you think her life is worth my time? Obviously, my brother's life wasn't worth your time, right? Maybe I should shoot her and leave her for dead like you left my brother."

"Look, all I was tryin' do was hit a come up, and that's what the fuck I did. I ain't give a fuck whose brother that nigga was. You ain't supposed to give a fuck about shit when you hungry, and that night, I was starvin', nigga."

Xae clenched his jaw tightly and then relaxed his broad stance. "I was gon' let her live, but you keep talkin' to me like that, and maybe I'll change my mind."

"Go get my fuckin' daughter, nigga, before I stop playin' nice," I said through gritted teeth.

We both still hand our guns in hand, one just waiting for the other to make the wrong move or say the wrong shit. I decided long before meeting with his ass that I was gon' make it out with my kid. I ain't give a fuck how I had to do it. I didn't go there to lose nothin' else. Xae turned his head to Bria and nodded. As soon as she got close enough to me, I grabbed her and quickly held my gun to her head.

"Move, and I'll shoot her in her mothafuckin' face, nigga!" I yelled. "You know what, nah, that's too easy," I said, lowering my gun to her stomach.

Without a second thought, I clutched the trigger and let my gun sound off. I watched Xae's hard demeanor melt like a popsicle on a hot summer day as he watched her fall to the ground. "Now you know how it feels to have your mothafuckin' child taken from you, nigga."

I didn't even give Xae a chance to take his next breath. Gunshots echoed within the walls as I reloaded my gun, cocked it back and fired in his direction and then again at her. I could see blood leaking from both of their bodies, but it wasn't good enough for me. They deserved to suffer for what they put me and my entire family through. I stepped closer. Blood splattered up on my face and clothes as I stood over them both and shot until my clip was empty.

"Now we even, bitch," I mumbled at the two dead mothafuckas layin' at my feet.

I reached down to retrieve the bag of money and Pharaoh's drugs. My boots kicked up dust as I ran into the room and saw Imani lying on an old mattress sleeping soundly. Worry suddenly snaked through me. I didn't want her to have seen or heard anything I'd done to get her back. She was too young to understand that sometimes you had to sacrifice a life or two to save one.

"Baby girl? Wake up, baby girl," I whispered in her ear.

I watched her closely as her eyes slowly opened, and she looked at me. "D-daddy?"

"It's me, baby girl."

"I wanna go home," she whispered.

I scooped her shivering body into my arms, and from that moment on, vowed to never let her go again. "Shh, it's okay, baby girl. Daddy's here."

ELITE

I woke up to see Frenchie standing in the doorway of my bedroom with Imani sleeping in his arms. Within seconds, I pulled her into my arms and cradled her. "Oh my God, my baby," I cried. "Is she okay, Frenchie? Is she hurt?"

"No."

"Let's go."

"Go where?"

"We need to take her to the hospital to be fully checked out."

"I got business to handle, Elite. I just wanted to bring her home to you like I told you I would."

I put her down on my bed and turned to Frenchie. "Thank you for bringing her back," I told him as I wrapped my arms around him.

His cold body pressed into mine, and he held me tight. "I will do anything to make this right," he whispered in my ear.

Tears seeped out of my eyes, and I couldn't figure out if they were tears of joy, pain, relief, or a mixture of all four. I felt like I was in the middle of a dream that I was scared to wake up from. I closed my eyes and then opened them again just to be sure that Imani was asleep on my bed where she should've been all along, and I was wrapped in Frenchie's arms.

For those few minutes, everything in my life was truly

perfect. It was something that I thought I'd never feel again.

AS SOON AS the sun rose the next morning, I packed up Imani and Paxton in the car and headed straight to the emergency room to get Imani checked out from head to toe. I was relieved to learn that she was fine. Before we left, I got the call that Pharaoh needed someone to pick him up and take him home. As soon as I opened the door to his hospital room, Imani ran in and jumped on his bed.

"Uncle P!" she squealed.

"Easy, Imani!" I told her before she jumped into his arms.

He looked at her with wide eyes and a smile across his face. "Baby girl, I missed you!"

"Are you okay?"

"Yeah, I'm going to be fine."

"What happened to you?"

"Somebody tried to hurt me," he told her.

"They shot you?"

I looked at Pharaoh and then back at Imani. "Yeah, they did," he said.

"Everything good?" I chimed in.

"Yeah. Everything is good on that end?"

"Yes."

"They took the dirty clothes to the cleaners?"

"As far as I know."

He nodded. "Good."

"So, I heard you're breaking out of here today, and you need a getaway car." I chuckled.

"Yeah, I'm ready to get up out of here. I already signed my discharge papers and everything. I'm good to go."

Pharaoh held Imani's hand as I carried Paxton out to the car. Once everyone was strapped in, I backed out of the parking spot and started driving Pharaoh home.

"So what's goin' on with you and French?" he asked me.

"Shh, ears back there."

"My fault."

I shrugged. "I don't know. Sometimes I feel like I could love him to death, other times it's like I could never speak to him and I wouldn't lose a wink of sleep over it."

"Damn."

"What about you?" I asked.

"What about me?"

"You know what... Have you talked to... Savannah, right?"

"Nah, not since I woke up in the hospital and she was there."

"I know you're not one to take anyone's advice, but I'm going to give you my two cents anyway. I think you should."

"Is that right?"

"Yeah."

"And why is that?"

"If not for anything else, closure. I know you still think about her. As closed as you pretend you are, she's got you wide open. Lord knows people make mistakes, Pharaoh. It would be a shame if you missed out on a good girl just because of a mistake."

"What makes you so sure any of it was a mistake?"

"If she didn't care about you, do you think she would've showed to Imani's birthday party? Or saved your life? Riot told us the whole story about what happened at the club that night. Believe it or not, women aren't aliens. We want simple shit, and we do simple shit. It doesn't take a rocket scientist to know that she loves you."

He shook his head as if he disagreed with me. "That's what you think, huh?"

"I'm a woman, Pharaoh, so it's not what I think; it's what I know."

Little did he know, I was speaking to him from experience. I didn't know what kind of woman Savannah was, but if she had any of the good qualities Michael had, I knew she was the type of woman that Pharaoh needed in his life. Their situation was totally different from mine. They didn't have the same strings holding them back.

The car fell silent, and all we could hear was the sound of the radio. "Well, if I gotta talk to her, then you gotta talk to you know who."

I sucked my teeth. "Really?"

"Yeah, really."

"I don't know how that's going to go. Don't get me wrong, I'm happy as hell to have my baby back, but at the same time, none of this would've ever happened if it weren't for his moves."

"I feel you. We both know what he did was wrong, and it put a lot of people in jeopardy, but he knows he fucked up, Elite."

"I stuck by your cousin when he had next to nothing in his wallet, through the cheating, everything. I gave him the kids that he begged me for, and what do I have to show for it? All this talk about him wanting his family back but can never stop himself from entertaining the next bitch. I'm tired of him dragging me through the mud."

"What do you need from him? Tell me."

"What do I need from him? I need him to be a grateful ass nigga and finally realize what he had instead of adding unnecessary stress to my life. I need him to handle the highs and lows of life with maturity, and not try to spend the day with his head in the clouds. I need him to stop giving the attention he should be giving me to other females. I want to be his wife not his mother, you know? If the effort isn't there, then I can't be either."

"Hold up, you said you want to be his wife, like in present tense."

I bit my bottom lip. He'd caught me. "Shit, I would probably be happily married by now if I wasn't in love with a hood ass nigga."

"You probably right." He chuckled.

"I'll talk to him, but I swear to you, he's going to have to move heaven and Earth to win me back. I'm not playing around this time."

It was the first time I'd come out and was able to accurately put what I wanted into words that made sense outside of my head. If Pharaoh ever relayed my message to Frenchie, I was curious to see if it changed him.

Chapter Ten

SAVANNAH

I'd cried buckets of tears over losing out on the possibility of having anything with Pharaoh again. Regret loomed over my head like a gray cloud, and it was finally time I stopped torturing myself by chasing Pharaoh, literally and figuratively. I had to face the fact that happily ever after didn't exist with street niggas, and that the chapter of my life was over. He and I were two pieces of the puzzle that just didn't fit.

With that thought in the forefront of my mind, I continued packing up everything I had to head back to D.C. With a handful of clothes in my hand, I heard a knock at the door. Thinking nothing of it, I put the clothes down and swung the door open and stood there staring straight into Pharaoh's eyes. There was an immediate rush of feelings pinging from my brain, to my heart and down to the soles of my feet.

"Pharaoh, w-what are you doing here? When you'd get out of the hospital?"

"Yesterday."

"How are you feeling?"

"I'm aight."

"How'd you get in the building?"

"Damn, what's with all the questions? I followed somebody in."

"I didn't mean anything by it. You showing up here just caught me by surprise," I told him.

"Did I catch you at a bad time?"

I shook my head. "Oh, um, no. Come in."

I stepped to the side and watched him walk past me. The

way he looked at me made my body tingle with heat as if my entire body had been set on fire. I could barely stand it. When it came to him, I was so fragile it was painful. He walked into the living room and saw the two large suitcases open on the floor.

"Going somewhere?"

I shrugged with my hands in my back pockets. "Finally decided to give you what you wanted and head back to D.C."

"When?"

"My train leaves in three hours," I told him.

He smiled sadly as if he would miss me. "So this is good-bye, huh?"

"Yeah, I guess it is. I'm not ready to take a flight back to D.C., so the train is the next best thing."

"Or you could stay…"

I frowned. "Aren't you the one who told me Chicago was too small for the both of us?"

He smiled at the fact that I'd used his own words against him and leaned against the countertop in the kitchen. "You and that smart ass mouth."

"What are you really doing here?" I asked, folding my arms loosely across my chest. "Because if you came to tell me you don't love me, or you want me to stay away from you, then I'm sorry. You wasted your time coming all the way over here. This is me finally giving you what you want," I said, pointing to the half-filled suitcases.

"Nah, I didn't come here for all that."

"Then what is it?"

I shifted my weight from one foot to the other. Having Pharaoh in my presence made me nervous. It felt like a permanent caffeine buzz flowing through me.

"What time does your train leave again?" he asked.

"In three hours."

"Ride with me somewhere. I wanna show you something."

"I don't think we have enough time. I'm nowhere near done packing."

"Do you trust me?"

I pressed my lips in a hard line and nodded. "Yeah, I do."

"Then just come with me, Savannah."

I looked at him with pause. There was something different in the way he looked at me. It was the first time in what felt like forever that his eyes were soft, calm even. I nodded, grabbed my keys, and followed him outside. When I closed the passenger door to Pharaoh's midnight black Mercedes, he drove off. He took the exit onto the interstate and immediately slowed down. Cars were honking as they lined up bumper to bumper in traffic.

"Where exactly are we going?" I asked.

"I thought you said you trusted me."

"Yeah, but by the looks of this traffic, I feel like I'm going to be late."

"Just sit back and relax."

Once we finally got out of traffic, Pharaoh drove another thirty minutes and then pulled his car up to a construction site. I looked around at the stacks of lumber lying next to the framework of a large house or building being built. There was tarp covering some of the supplies and new windows with stickers still attached to them.

"What is this?" I asked.

"Get out of the car."

I rolled my eyes and then got out and followed him toward what would eventually be the main entrance of the building. We both kicked up a light cloud of sawdust under our feet on the way inside. Everything smelled new.

"Are you going to tell me what all this is now?" I asked again.

"It's my way out."

"Your what?"

"You remember when I told you that I wanted to give back to my city?"

I nodded. "Yeah."

"Well, this is the first of many."

"What is it?"

"When it's finished, it'll be the Gladys Blackwell Community Center."

"Who is that?" I asked.

"Big Mama, my grandmother. It was her dream to do something for the community. I just adopted it when she died. This is my way of giving back on her behalf and making up for all the times I let her down."

My eyes softened as I gazed at him. "Wow, Pharaoh. That's really amazing."

"Thank you."

He walked over to the granite countertop and unfolded the blueprint to show me what the place would look like when it was done. It was going to have three full-size basketball courts, large community rooms for meetings, an auditorium, two Olympic-sized swimming pools, and more. I was in awe at how much thought he'd put into it all.

"This is all great, but how can you afford all of this after everything they took from you?"

"I'm from the hood. Where I come from, we don't trust the bank to hold all our shit."

"So nothing happened to your money?"

"Not even."

"What about your house?"

"I'm good. For one, I got a dope ass lawyer, and for two, I'm way smarter than even the Feds. I've always been a student of the game."

I looked back at him and flashed a smile. "So you're just that nigga, huh?"

"A nigga not just guns and drugs like how you thought I was. I can be a dope nigga and a humble one at the same time." I chuckled.

"I may have thought that once, but I know you're so much more than that... But why
show me any of it when you know I'm leaving?"

He rubbed the back of his neck and then looked at me. "I

had no intention of talking to you again, but seeing you with your bags... I don't know. I guess I'm not as ready to let you go as I thought I was," he confessed.

My heart did a somersault in my chest and then plummeted to the pit of my stomach.

"I brought you here to tell you that I heard you at the hospital."

"You were awake, so I know you did."

"Nah, I mean, really heard you."

"What does that mean?"

"It means I fuckin' loved you, Savannah!"

"Loved?" I asked with a hint of sadness in my voice.

"I remember the first time I saw you in that hospital. Your smile. The innocent look on your face with the hint of confusion when you saw me. The way your fuckin' eyes danced when you laughed. I couldn't get you off my mothafuckin' mind after that... and I still can't."

Before I had the chance to respond, I felt Pharaoh's lips lightly brush against mine. Every bone in my body was on fire with passion. His kiss was so intense that my nails clung to his shoulders, never wanting his body to drift even a centimeter away from mine. We slowly pulled away, panting, unable to catch our breaths.

"I love you, Savannah."

PHARAOH

The longer I stood around Savannah, the faster I could feel myself breaking down. Giving in, bit by bit. Piece by fuckin' piece. I'd buried my heart six feet under, and she brought it back to the surface with ease. If she was going to leave and never step foot in Chicago again, I had to make sure that she didn't go without knowing how I truly felt about her. I was going to make sure she had a night that she'd never forget. We stood close with our foreheads pressed together, taking in everything about the other's presence, from the passion flickering in her eyes to the skipping rhythm of her heartbeat.

She stared at me breathlessly with glistening eyes. "Tell me again," she whispered.

I gently held the sides of her face and looked into her eyes. "I love you."

A light smile creased her lips, followed by her eyes telling me to kiss her again, so I did. When I pulled away again, she flashed her eyes up at me. "What made you finally say it back?"

"I got tired of fighting it."

"So are we officially starting over?" she asked.

"I guess so."

"Clean slate?"

"Yeah."

"Truth?"

"Nothin' but."

I knew Savannah and I had a long road ahead of us. We were going to have to learn to trust each other all over again. She was who I wanted to be with. No one else even came close. She turned around to look at the blueprint again, and I pulled her close to me. I pulled her hair to one side as I kissed on her neck from behind. Her body was immediately responsive to my touch. I felt her knees turn to water as I gently ran my fingers through her hair and drew in her scent. She smelled like a mixture of lavender and vanilla.

"Damn, you don't know how much I missed you," I whispered against her skin.

"Then show me…"

Savannah turned to me and peeled her jacket off her shoulders. She tossed it to the floor, and I reached out to slide the straps of her tank top and bra down and took her breasts in my hand. With my hands wrapped around her waist, I picked her up and laid her against the countertop, pushing the blueprint off to the side. My lips kissed from hers down to her chest as I sucked on each nipple. Her mouth gaped open in pleasure as her fingertips combed through my hair. Unable to hold back, I pulled down her sweatpants and panties at the same time and started tongue fucking her pussy.

"Ooh fuck," she moaned as my hands held her thighs suspended in the air.

She watched me snake my tongue against her pussy and squirmed in pleasure underneath my grasp. I sucked on my fingertips and then inserted my middle finger inside of her. Her body tensed and then released. Before she had a chance to cum, I slid my dick through the hole in my boxers and pushed inside her for a few strokes.

"Ooooh my God!" She shivered.

I watched her caramel-colored nipples wet from my tongue, bounce with every stroke as her hair hung off the edge of the countertop. I looked at her as if I owned every part of her. She was mine, and I would never let her go. I would give her good love and good dick for the rest of my days.

Her lips were paralyzed in an O-shape as I leaned in to cut off her moans with a kiss. My tongue played tag with hers for a few strokes until I pulled out and licked her pussy again, vibrating my long tongue against her sweet spot. I could taste her cream on my tongue. I slid off my pants and boxers and saw the head of my dick was white from her cum. Once I slid back inside her, her body became loose, shapeless like water, bending into any position my hands welded her into. With my hands locked underneath her ass, I thrusted upward inside her while swiveling my hips in slow circles. Her body tensed as her nails dug into my forearms.

"Mmm, right there, Pharaoh, baby!"

I lifted her off the countertop and let her ride me while I held her suspended in the air.

She rocked back and forth with her arms wrapped around me, moaning in my ear. "Oh my God, yes. I missed you so much, baby."

I grabbed her by the throat and kissed her hard while putting her down so that her feet were back on the floor. Savannah continued to breath out moans, even when I wasn't penetrating her. I slid two fingers inside her warmth and finger fucked her to her climax before she dropped down to her knees. She looked up at me as she wrapped her lips around the tip of my dick. Savannah licked up the shaft and then sucked on the head like a lollipop. I pushed her head down deeper as she sucked my dick harder. I used my other hand to pull her hair into a ponytail as she pulled her lips further onto my piece.

"Mmm, shit," I groaned as my hands palmed the back of her head.

Savannah sucked harder and faster like she was trying to make me feel how sorry she was.

"Yeah, wet that shit up, Savannah," I growled.

As soon as I felt my toes start to curl underneath me, I slowly stepped back. I helped her back up to her feet and then spun her around and bent her over the countertop. My kisses traced from the back of her neck and shoulders all the way down her spine. When my lips touched the tip of the spread of her ass, I pushed inside her from behind.

"Mmm," I groaned against her back.

She pushed her hair to the side as her fingertips gripped the countertop. "Yes, baby," she whispered.

I thrusted my hips forward while kneading her nipples between my finger. "Just like that?"

"Harder!"

"Mmm, you want it harder?" I asked, pounding my dick into her so hard I thought she was going to explode.

"Yes, baby! It feels soooo good!"

"I'm the only nigga you love?" I asked.

"Yes, baby, only you!"

The deeper I swam in her pussy, the juicier she got. I smacked her bronzed ass while finessing her body straight into euphoric pleasure. The louder she moaned, the stronger the tingling sensation got in the soles of my feet. I hovered over her as my last few strokes sent me over the edge.

"Mmm, shit!" I groaned.

After we caught our breaths and got redressed, we headed back outside to my car. As soon as I started the engine, she turned her head to me. "These are the moments I crave," she said.

"What do you mean?"

"From the moment I met you, I started to crave the most vulnerable parts of you. The parts you only show me when we're alone."

I could see the vulnerability in her eyes. "Why do you love me?" I asked.

"It's not because of who you are or what you do, but how you make me feel. You ignite things in me that I never even knew existed. You took my heart before I even had the chance to stop you. I fell in love with who you showed me you were, and who you showed me I can be. I just love every part of you, Pharaoh," she told me.

"I love you, too."

Chapter Eleven

ELITE

It had been about a week and a half since Frenchie got Imani back. I'd agreed to move back into the house to make sure Imani felt as if nothing had changed in her home life since she'd been away, and she seemed to be adjusting well. I slept upstairs with Imani in my bed every night, while Frenchie agreed to either sleep downstairs on the couch or in the basement. As grateful as I was to have her back, it hadn't changed much about how I felt toward Frenchie. I was happy to have him around to help me with the kids again, but I was still mad at him for everything he'd put us through. I didn't know if I'd ever be able to let it go.

I woke up the next morning for work, when I heard "Anniversary" by Tony, Toni, Tone blasting through the speakers in the living room. I opened my bedroom door and walked down the stairs and into the kitchen to see Frenchie in there.

"Good morning," he said, standing shirtless by the coffee maker.

"Um, good morning," I said with skepticism in my tone.

"I made you some coffee."

"Frenchie, what are you doing? You're never up this early."

"Do you know what today is?" He sang along with the song as he looked at me.

My forehead creased in confusion as I shifted my weight to one foot trying to recall the date. After a few seconds passed, it hit me. It was what would've been our seven-year anniversary if we'd still been together. "I know what it is."

"Then sing the song with me, girl."

"Cut that off, Frenchie."

He pressed the pause button on his phone, and the room fell silent. "C'mon, I was just tryna make you smile."

"Why?"

"Because you deserve it," he told me.

I flashed my eyes up at him. I knew he was trying, but I just didn't know why. "What are you up to?"

"I'm not up to nothin'."

"I already know you are, so you might as well go on and tell me."

"Aight, it's simple."

"What?"

"Have dinner with me tonight."

"What? No, Frenchie."

"Yes, Elite. Please."

I sucked my teeth. "No, because that means I have to find somebody to watch the kids."

"Already taken care of. Your mom already agreed to watch them."

I huffed. "Where we goin'?"

"It's a surprise. Just make sure you leave the shop in time to be ready by eight o'clock tonight."

WHEN I GOT HOME from work later that evening, Frenchie nor the kids were anywhere in sight. Once I called my mom to confirm that they were with her, I took my time alone to take a nice, long shower with no interruptions. I came out the bathroom wrapped in my towel and went into my closet to pick out what I was going to wear. I had no idea what Frenchie had up his sleeve, but it had been so long since I'd had the opportunity to dress up and go out, I wasn't going to let it pass me by. Once I settled on a strappy red bodycon dress with heels, I started to get dressed. As I was touching up the last curl on my hair, I heard keys jingling in the lock downstairs.

"Elite? You ready?" Frenchie yelled upstairs.

"Yeah, give me a second!" I yelled back.

I tucked some hair behind my ear, smoothed my hands

down the front of my dress, and headed down the stairs. He looked me up and down and licked his lips. "Damn."

"What?"

"You look perfect."

I cracked a slight smile. "Thank you... You clean up nice yourself," I said, noticing the crisp button up and dark denim jeans he was wearing as I stood there eyeing the dozen red roses in his hand. "Are those for me?"

"Oh, damn, yeah. These are for you."

He handed them to me, and I buried my nose in the fresh bouquet. "I don't think you've ever bought me flowers before."

"As good as you look tonight, I'll buy your ass a whole fuckin' garden."

I shook my head with a smile. "So where are we going?"

"All you need to know is I'm taking you somewhere nice that you've never been before. Now c'mon."

FRENCHIE PULLED UP in front of the Chicago Stock Exchange building, and I looked at him bewildered. "We're eating here?"

"Yes, this is where we're having dinner."

"Here? I heard you had to book reservations weeks in advance."

"You do."

"So how'd you get us reservations?"

"I threatened the owner." He shrugged.

I frowned. "What?"

"Relax, Elite. Now c'mon."

My heels clicked swiftly against the marble floor of the building as I followed Frenchie into the elevator. We rode it up to the fortieth floor to eat at the restaurant there. I still couldn't believe what we were doing in a ten-star restaurant. As we were taken to our table, I let myself sink into the scenery around us. The noise level was low, even with all the different types of people dining alongside us. There were two candles flickering on the table when we sat down. The dim lighting of the restaurant was the perfect contrast against the beautiful view of the city.

My ears perked up to the sound of the melodic piano music playing through the overhead speakers just as the waiter returned with menus. "Can I get you two something to drink?"

"I'll just take a glass of your house white wine," I told him.

"Nah, order what you want. I got you, Elite."

My lips twisted into a slight smile, and I nodded. "Well, I guess I'll have..."

"Can we get a bottle of your best champagne?"

"Right away, sir."

"Champagne, huh?" I asked as I adjusted the strap of my dress and glanced across the table at him. Frenchie wasn't a suit and tie type of nigga, but he still looked as crisp as a white-collar worker.

"Only the best tonight."

"What exactly are we celebrating?"

"I thought you said you remembered."

"I know what today is, Frenchie. I just don't know why you're doing all this when we're not even together," I told him.

"Look, Elite. I'm able to swallow my pride and tell you that I fucked up. I can't keep telling you how sorry I am. Now instead of telling you, I'm tryna show you, that's all."

I wanted to believe him, trust him, but I just wasn't sure. Silence hung awkwardly in between us, and I glanced over at the fancy embroidered curtains on the far side of the restaurant. We sat across from one another, diverting our eyes from landing on the other's.

"Your champagne," the waiter said as he placed the ice bucket with the champagne inside it on the table, and it wobbled underneath us. I giggled.

"As expensive as this damn menu is, you'd think they'd have tables with even legs," Frenchie said.

I smiled. "I know, right."

I was happy the uneven table leg was able to break the ice

again. Frenchie had never made me nervous in the past, but I was shaking like a virgin schoolgirl in his presence. There was a different vibe about him. He was confident, and I could see the clarity in his eyes. The waiter came back with two salads and placed them in front of us. We took turns placing our orders, and then he scurried away again. I placed the white napkin in my lap and crunched a few pieces of the salad between my teeth.

"You know... I really didn't know what to expect when you asked me to come to dinner."

"Are you enjoying yourself?" he asked.

"To be honest with you, I don't know yet."

"You don't know?"

"I'm still trying to figure out your motive."

"I told you, all I'm tryna do is treat you like the queen you are, Elite. When you left, all a nigga could do was sit and fuckin' think."

"About what?"

"About you, me, the kids, everything. Like I told you, I know I fucked up, but I guess I was too preoccupied with myself to think about how all the shit I was doing was affecting you."

I sighed. "I never asked you for expensive bouquets of roses or trips overseas, Frenchie. I asked you for the simplest forms of love, and you couldn't even give me that. I wanted you to tell me to have a great day. I wanted to hear you tell me you loved me without saying it during an argument or fucking. I'm a woman, Frenchie, not an alien. I'm not that hard to understand."

"That's the thing about me, Elite. I ain't never really known love, at least not how you wanted me to. The streets taught me love, so when I love, I love hard. Recklessly. Wrong," he confessed.

"I can't keep trying to teach you how to love me, Frenchie."

"Tell me how you want it. I'll give it to you anyway you need it." Like a fiend, I stared at his champagne-wet lips as he spoke. "Why don't you have a real drink with me?"

I shook my head. "I need to have a clear head around you."

"Why is that? Don't trust yourself?"

"I don't trust you."

He frowned. "I know, and I'm tryna work on that. I never want you to feel less than ever again. You deserve to be treated like every day is your birthday. These hoes ain't fuckin' with you, period. You are the total package. I just never bothered to see it until it was too late."

I took a quick glance at him. "Why'd you really come to see me that night?"

"Because I love you, and to be honest, there was a part of me that thought I was gonna die. I wanted you to be safe. After all that Imani shit, I made a promise on my life that I was going to keep you and my kids safe in this life and the next."

He was saying all the things my heart had longed to hear for years. I couldn't deny the growing magnetic attraction I started to feel toward him, but it was going to take a while before I trusted him with my heart again, not to mention my body.

"How can I trust that you'll do the right thing by me and the kids?" I asked.

"You just gotta let me show you. I miss lovin' the shit out of you. I need you right here by my side just like my gun is."

I set my eyes on the flickering candle flame in front of me and didn't give him an immediate response. Instead, I let my mind get carried away with thoughts of his cocoa brown skin pressed against mine. After twenty minutes, the waiter arrived with our food, and we started to eat.

THE TWO OF us walked over to the elevator, and he scooped my hand into his. My shoulders tensed then relaxed as I leaned my back against the elevator wall. Frenchie's tall stature hovered inches over me, even with heels on. He looked down at me and brought his lips toward mine. I gently turned my head.

"I'm not ready..." I whispered.

He lifted my hand to his lips and kissed it. "Mmm, I still remember the way you taste," he whispered.

We stood frozen until the elevator stopped on the first

floor and the doors opened. "After you."

I stepped out and walked back outside of the building to face the cold air head on. Once we got back inside his car, he turned the heat on full blast, and I blew heat into my hands. My eyes quickly darted over in his direction, scanning his body from head to toe.

"Thank you for dinner."

"Did you enjoy yourself?" he asked.

"I did."

"Good. That's all I wanted. I know this shit seems like it's coming out of left field, but I really am trying to show you that I can do right by you and my kids."

I nodded. "I know, and I do appreciate you for it... but I do have something I've been wanting to ask you."

"What is it?"

"The coke... are you still doing it?"

"I haven't done it in weeks. I was in a real bad space when I got on that shit, you know? I just wasn't tryna really deal with shit, which only made things worse."

"So you're completely clean?"

He shrugged. "As long as you don't count the weed."

I nodded and turned my attention out of the window. I was glad to hear that he'd stopped doing the hard drugs. I knew he was never going to stop smoking, so I didn't even bother to trip off that.

"Now that you got that off your chest, I got a question for you."

"Okay..."

"Did you ever fuck with another nigga?"

My eyes widened. "What?"

"Hear me out."

"Why would you ask me that?" I asked defensively.

"There was a time when I felt like the reason you weren't fuckin' with me was because you were fuckin' with another nigga."

"Frenchie, I—"

"All I'm sayin' is, even if you did step out on me, I'd be mad, but I know there's a part of me that can't blame you. Just know that I'm gon' always be your nigga, Elite, whether we together or not."

"You sound crazy when you say shit like that," I told him.

"I am crazy. Shit, being around you drives me fuckin' crazy, but being without you drives me crazy, too. I love you, girl."

The thought of saying it back bounced around in my head, but I held back. I unhooked my seat belt and pulled my keys out of my clutch as I walked up to the front door. As soon as I got into the house, I scampered over to the couch and wrapped my body in a blanket. Frenchie followed me inside and locked the door behind him. He walked over and plopped down on the couch beside me, while turning on the TV.

"Can you do me a favor?" I asked.

"What?"

"Unhook my shoes. My feet are really starting to kill me."

He reached down to grab my feet and put them in his lap. Each heel dropped to the floor as he gently kneaded the soles of my feet with his hands. I could slowly feel my body warming up and sinking deeper into the cushions of the couch. I'd gone from standing on my feet at the shop all day to putting on heels and going to dinner with Frenchie. My dogs were barking, and his massage was just what the doctor had ordered. I closed my eyes and let the talking heads on the TV lull me to sleep.

"Damn, girl. Is the massage that good, or I'm just boring?" he asked, making me reopen my eyes.

"I'm so tired, Frenchie. I'm about to head upstairs and go to bed. Goodnight."

"Can I come up?" he asked.

I sucked my teeth. "Up? What you wanna come up for, Frenchie?"

"To tuck the kids in goodnight, that's all."

"Nice try. You know damn well the kids are at my mama's house tonight."

"Then let me tuck you in then, Elite..."

FRENCHIE

I knew what I said to her had her stuck, but I missed everything about her. She stood up from the couch, and I stood up with her. I reached out and ran my fingertips down the seam of her dress as I looked her up and down with lustful eyes.

"Frenchie, I don't wanna—"

"Shh," I said as I gently kissed her red painted lips.

I felt Elite's body sink into mine as I ran my hands over her ass, lifted her dress, and pulled at her lace panties.

"Frenchie, stop," she whispered as she moved my hands

away and adjusted her dress.

I stepped back and wiped my hand down my lips and beard. "I'm sorry."

Elite brushed past me, and I turned to watch her walk upstairs. I stood in the middle of the living room floor until I heard the bedroom door close. I massaged my hard dick through my pants, hoping it would go down quick. After pulling off my shirt, pants, and shoes, I slid on some basketball shorts and laid down on the couch. I could hear Elite's footsteps pacing back and forth between the bedroom and the bathroom. All I wanted to do was please her, but she had put up a brick wall between us and wasn't allowing me the opportunity to knock it down. As soon as my eyes closed, I heard Elite scream. My body shot up, and I headed for the stairs.

"Elite? You aight?" I asked, jiggling the doorknob to the bedroom door.

She ran over to open it with a distressed look across her face. "There's a fuckin' spider in the shower!"

I burst out laughing then shook my head. "Damn, girl. You had me really thinkin' some shit was actually wrong."

"Come kill it!"

I walked into the closet to grab a shoe, then headed into the bathroom to kill the spider. Once I picked it up with some toilet paper and flushed it down the toilet, I turned to see her standing in the doorway. "It's dead," I assured her.

She sighed. "Thank you. There I was, about to take a fuckin' shower, and as soon as I pulled the curtain back, there his big ass was!"

"It really wasn't that big. You're just being dramatic." I laughed.

She rolled her eyes. "Yeah, whatever. Thank you though."

"Anything else you need before I go?"

"Um… no, I think I'm good."

"Yeah? You sure?"

"What is it that you're really trying to get me to say, Frenchie?"

"That you want a nigga as bad as I want you." She rolled her eyes again. "You know you want some anniversary dick."

"Maybe I do, but we not together, remember?"

"We can be just for the night if you want," I said, stepping closer to her.

Her head shook slowly from left to right as she watched me reach out and grab the sides of her face. I gently placed my lips on hers. The kiss was sloppy. It was unplanned. It was us.

"I still remember fuckin' you slow," I whispered in her ear while planting kisses all over her neck.

Her knees buckled underneath her as I backed her out of the bathroom and up against the bed. I pulled my dick out of my shorts and let her massage it while I ran my fingers through her hair. I was giving her the true hood affection her body craved. With a quick thrust, I lifted her body onto the bed and peeled her dress off.

Elite propped herself up on her elbows while spreading her smooth thighs. I locked my hands underneath the bend of her knees and licked her pussy slowly before burying my lips against her skin. Her cocoa brown skin felt like pure golden honey against my lips.

"Mmm, I love the way you taste, Elite," I mumbled against her clit.

I licked my fingertips and rubbed them against her pussy in slow circles, then slid two fingers inside her warmth as I licked and sucked on her clit. I started writing my name with my tongue against her flesh to remind her whose pussy it was.

"Ahhh shit, baby," she moaned as she lifted her neck then tossed her head back against the bed.

"Come ride my fuckin' face," I demanded.

Once I was on my back, Elite straddled my face and started bouncing her ass back against my lips as I sucked on her clit. I gripped her ass with my fingertips and sloppily licked her pussy from left to right and up and down, side to side.

"Mmm, fuck!"

She looked back at me with an expression mixed of pleasure and pain written across her face. She didn't want me to stop. She wanted me to keep going and going and going until I couldn't go anymore. I turned her around so that I could look up at her. She ran her fingers through her hair as she looked down at me. I reached up to massage her titties, jiggling them in my hands as she bucked forward, harder and harder. In slow circles, broken, rhythmless grinds just to cum. Anything that felt good to her, felt good to me. I glanced up and watched her eyes roll back inside her head as she squeezed her eyes closed.

"Oh my God, yes! Yes!"

Her mouth hung ajar as she came hard, leaving my lips and beard a wet, sticky mess. I smacked my lips against her clit one more time before letting her climb down. She grabbed my dick like she missed it, and I smiled.

"You gon' let me ride it?"

"I let you ride it long as you want to," I said while grabbing a hand full of her ass.

I gripped her waist as she slowly eased her wetness down onto my dick. Her mouth opened, and then she quickly sunk her teeth into her bottom lip. I spread her ass cheeks apart to make sure she felt every inch of me inside her. The second she started to ride it like the pro she was, I knew I had her hooked on my dick like phonics. I'd never seen her look more beautiful than she did while making her sex faces.

I growled with pleasure. "I can hear your pussy callin' for daddy."

"Mmhm!"

Elite continued to ride my dick as I massaged her jiggling titties in the palms of my hands. After she'd busted her first nut, I lifted her off me and flipped her over onto her back for the next position. She flashed her eyes up at me with passion flickering in them. I brushed my hard dick against the slit of her pussy, then grabbed the head and pushed inside. I held her legs wide open and watched my dick snake in and out of her.

"Ooh yes, baby! You're gonna make me squirt!"

"Squirt all on this dick!"

I leaned in to suck on her nipples then licked my finger-tips and rubbed them against her clit while I fucked her.

"Yessss, baby! Just like that!" she screamed.

"You like that shit?"

"Yes! Your dick is so amazing, baby!"

I fucked her until her pussy squirted all over my dick, and then slid out of her and turned her body over so that she was face down in the sheets. After propping her ass up just how I wanted it, I pushed back past her walls and gripped her ass. "Mmm, fuck, Elite."

I brushed my thumb against her asshole as I fucked her from behind. It didn't take long before she started bucking back against me and making her ass jiggle.

"Yeah, pop that ass back on this dick," I said as I yanked her hair back like her back didn't have any bones.

I pulled her arms behind her back, holding her wrists tight as I fucked her fast. She started to scream so loud I knew she could be heard from all the way outside.

"Tell me how you want it," I said as I ran my fingertips down the curve of her back.

"Deeper, baby!"

"Mmm, you want me to put it all in?"

"Yes!"

"Can you take it? Hmm?"

"Yes, baby, I can take it!"

The deeper I stroked, the louder she got. I knew her screams could be heard from all the way outside the house. After a few more strokes, I gave in to the tightness of her pussy and let it drain my dick. I let out a low groan from deep within me and fell back against the bed with my heart beating over a hundred beats per minute.

"Goddamn I missed you."

She ran her fingers through her hair. "I think maybe we both missed each other."

"Shit, after all that, you got a nigga mouth all dry and shit. I'm thirsty as hell."

"I'll go downstairs and get some water," she said.

"Nah, I got it."

"No, it's fine."

"Elite, I told you I got it."

"I'll race you down there," she said, jumping off the bed and getting a head start.

I had no idea how she had that much energy after the dick down I'd just given her, but I got up and headed for the door. I barely gave her any competition as her naked body ran down the stairs and into the kitchen to the fridge.

"I won!" She beamed.

"Only because I let you."

"Yeah, whatever," she said, smacking her lips.

Once we both got a few sips of cold water into our system, I reached out to smack her ass. "Go upstairs and put some clothes on unless you want a repeat of what just happened."

"Maybe a repeat would be good..." she said, eyeing me with the look in her eyes that told me she wanted to get shit started again.

"C'mon then."

"I'll go turn on the shower. Cut the lights off before you come back upstairs," she
said as she walked back up the stairs.

I turned the lamp off, and as soon as the lights went out, bullets lit up the entire front of my house. I heard Elite scream, and I ran in her direction. I got hit over three times and fell to the ground. I army crawled up the stairs and didn't stop until I covered Elite's body with my own. Bullets continued to fly out in rounds only semi-automatic weapons could produce. As soon as my life started flashing in front of my eyes, I knew I was going to die.

Chapter Twelve

ELITE

The paramedic slammed on the brakes as he pulled up underneath the awning of the emergency room. They hurriedly took Frenchie out and pushed his stretcher through the double doors. I was right behind them, holding his hand. "Just hold on, Frenchie, baby. Please, don't leave me!"

"I'm sorry, ma'am, but you can't go back with them," one of the nurses said, stopping me in my tracks.

Frenchie's hand slipped out of mine as the stretcher kept rolling through another set of double doors. "He needs me."

"The doctors will do everything they can for him."

"I—I can't leave him."

"I'm going to need you to wait in the waiting room like everyone else. I'll make sure he knows you're here as soon as I can."

She turned to walk away, and I headed into the waiting room. The television was on, blaring an old black and white movie. I plopped down into one of the hard, plastic chairs and pulled out my phone to call Pharaoh.

"Hello?" he answered.

As soon as I heard his voice, I burst into tears. "P…"

"Elite? What's wrong?"

"Fre-Frenchie got shot. I'm at th-the hospital. I don't think he's gonna make it, P. What am I gonna do if he dies, huh? What the fuck am I gonna tell my kids?" I cried.

"Don't worry about nothin'. Frenchie is a fighter. Stay there, aight? I'm on my way."

"Okay."

I buried my head in my hands as thousands of what if questions darted through my mind. What if my kids had been in the house? What if they would've shot and killed both Frenchie and me? I'd just gotten him back. I would lose my mind if I lost him so soon.

FRENCHIE

My eyes opened to see the tiled ceiling above me. The lights were so bright that I shuddered and quickly closed my eyes right back. There were tubes attached to my arms and underneath my nose, and I had no idea how I'd survived my house being shot up and my body being riddled with bullets. To the left of me was Elite sitting with all three of my kids by her side. I did my best to clear my throat before speaking.

"Baby?" I asked in a raspy voice.

"Oh my God, you're finally awake," she said, coming over to me and kissing the top of my head.

"Junior," I said, calling out to my oldest son. "How did he get here?" I asked Elite.

"Corinne dropped him off here for a few hours. I figured you'd want to see him whenever you got out of your surgery."

"Surgery?"

"Yeah..."

"I thought I died."

"You did."

"What?"

"The doctors told me you flatlined on the table, but they were able to bring you back and remove as many fragments of the bullets as possible, but they couldn't get them all."

I looked over at my kids, then down at the gown I was dressed in that smelled like seventy-five percent bleach and twenty-five percent detergent. "I'm ready to get out of here."

"I'm just so glad you're okay."

"Shit, me too."

"I really can't stand the thought of losing you, especially not like that."

"I've never felt that much pain in my life. It felt like I was crying blood. It hurt so bad."

"If it felt nearly as bad as it looked, I can only imagine."

"I just keep thinkin' if they took me out, who the fuck was gon' care after they dropped my casket into the ground?"

"I would care, Frenchie. You know I would."

"After all I did to you... I wouldn't be surprised if you didn't."

"Look, now isn't the time to talk about that, especially with extra ears in the room," she told me.

I nodded as my eyes gazed down to the slate gray floor. I'd lived by the gun for so long, it was only right that I died by that mothafucka, too. Fortunately, God had given me a second chance at life, and I would've been a fool to fuck that up. I took turns hugging and kissing each of my kids, then Elite. She'd showed me the true meaning of family, and I wanted mine back more than anything in the world.

"I just want my family back," I told her.

She pressed her lips together firmly. "Frenchie, I—"

"I will do anything to make you happy, Elite. You own my heart," I said, cutting her off.

I searched her eyes for an answer, and when I didn't get one, I fixated my attention to the dove white wall in front of me.

"Maybe we could try something on a trial basis... just to see how it goes. I'm not going to say no, but I'm also not going to jump head first into anything so soon. We have so much to figure out."

I nodded. "That's fair."

"First things first, we need to find a new place to live. I'm not letting my kids step foot back inside there ever again."

"Fuck that house. We can make new memories any-where," I assured her.

The door opened, and Pharaoh stood there with an un-easy look on his face. I waved him in, and he walked over to the side of my bed.

"Am I interrupting something important?" he asked.

I looked at Elite, and she shook her head. "Nah, it's cool. Yo, let me holla at my cousin real quick."

The two of us stood in silence as we watched Elite gather up the kids and step outside. Pharaoh turned to me and shook his head. "Yo, what the fuck happened?"

I shook my head. "I shoulda saw it comin'," I mumbled to him.

"I thought you told me shit was handled."

"It was... until it wasn't."

"Do you know who did the shit?" he asked, tightly grip-ping the arm empty chair beside him.

"Had to be that nigga Xae's brother on some retaliation shit."

"You sure?"

"Yeah. He was the nigga I robbed, then Xae stepped in on some big brother shit, and I killed his ass, so he's the only mothafucka left with a score to settle with my ass."

Xae was dead, but his brother wasn't, and since I wasn't either, that meant I had to finish that nigga before he finished me and my entire family.

PHARAOH

Just looking at my cousin laid up in a hospital bed, knowing shit could've went differently, had my blood boiling. The moment I heard that his house had gotten shot up, Frenchie's problems became my own. I was going to make sure the shit ended in blood.

"How'd you even know I was here?"

"Elite called and told me. She sounded so fucked up over the phone, I didn't know what the fuck I was about to walk into," I told him.

"I don't know why I was surprised to see her sitting here when I woke up. It's probably because I thought the next time I opened my eyes, I'd be sittin' in hell or somethin'," he told me.

"Thank God you still here, my nigga."

"Hell yeah, but since I am still here, it's time to get this mothafucka off my dick for good, you feel me?"

"I do."

"I'ma handle that shit as soon as I get out of this mothafuckin' hospital."

"Nah, I'ma handle it. For the family. You just focus on doin' what you gotta do to make sure you good. You got a girl and three kids to look after."

As much as I knew he wanted to fight me on it, he simply nodded. "For the family."

He dapped me up, and I took a seat in the chair next to him. "How you feelin'?"

"I don't know. To be honest, this shit still don't seem real to me. I don't know if it's the pain medication or what, but I'm just on one right now."

"That's how it is when you get shot. Trust me, that shit ain't no joke," I told him.

"You fuckin' right, nigga. I don't ever want to get shot again. If I do, the nigga better make sure he kill me with the first bullet. This suffering shit ain't no joke."

I nodded. "I feel you... I was happy to see Elite and the kids here though. How y'all doin' anyway?"

He shrugged. "We gettin' there, I guess. Just taking shit one day at a time."

"That's what's up, but real shit, if y'all are talkin' about gettin' back together, the first thing I'm gon' get your ass is a box of fuckin' condoms, nigga." I chuckled.

"I know."

"All bullshit aside, all she wants is for you to do right by her and all them damn kids you got, French. If you're serious about trying to get back with her, then you really gotta leave the bullshit in the past."

"Nigga, she told me I fuckin' died and came back to life. If that's not enough to make me get my shit together, then I don't know what is. I'ma do whatever the fuck I gotta do to make sure I don't hurt her again."

I nodded. "That's what's up."

LATER THAT NIGHT, I went back to the club where I'd seen Xae and some of his boys the first time. Once I got the girl Riot was fuckin' with to confirm that they were inside, I sat and waited in my car for an hour until the club let out.

"So you're really doing this?" Savannah asked me through the phone.

"Ain't got no choice."

"There's always a choice, Pharaoh."

"Not in this case."

She sighed. "I guess..."

"Don't start that shit with me right now. These niggas shot at me, and they shot up my fuckin' cousin's house. This shit is goin' to end tonight."

"I just want you to be safe, that's all."

"I will be. These mothafuckas aren't gon' catch me slippin' again."

"I love you..." she said sadly.

"Don't say it like that."

"Like what?"

"Like it's the last time you'll ever say it to me."

"I'm sorry. I just don't have a good feeling about this, especially with you going alone."

"I'll be fine. The club is letting out now. I gotta go. I'll call you later."

"Tell me you love me."

"I love you, Savannah," I said and hung up.

My eyes weeded through the sea of people until my eyes locked on Xae's brother. He was staggering out of the club with a girl attached to his arm. Just looking at him, I could tell he was on somethin', so I knew it would be easy for me to get to him. He got in the passenger seat of a black Mercedes and pulled off. I started the engine and then slowly pulled out behind him, being sure to stay a few car lengths behind.

I drove for another twenty minutes across the city until the car pulled up in front of a house and stopped. I couldn't see in the car because of the dark tint on the windows, so I drove past them and parked a little further down the road so that I could watch them through my rearview mirror. Xae's brother got out of the car and walked over to the driver's side. The bitch he was with rolled down the window and he leaned into to talk to her. After a few minutes, she drove off, and he zigzagged up the stairs, holding onto the railing for stability.

I got out of the car with my gun in my hand and pushed through the cold, whistling wind as I ran up on him. "Yo, you need some help?" I asked.

He shook his head. "Nah, mothafucka, I'm good. I don't know you."

The second he looked up at me, I cocked my gun in his face. Shock flooded his eyes when he realized who I was. "Surprise, mothafucka."

He pushed me away from him and tried to run up the stairs. As soon as he got to the front door, he heard my gun cock, then gunfire rang out. I shot him in the ankle and watched him fall to his knees. I ran up behind him, fished his keys out of his pocket, and dragged him inside the house. While he was down, I kicked him in his ribs then stood over him.

"You should have played your hand better, nigga. Tryna fuck with what we got, you ain't never gon' win, nigga. That's facts. You should've backed down when you had the chance."

"Fuck you, nigga. My brother should've killed you when he had the chance. You Blackwell niggas are like fuckin' roaches. He was my fuckin' blood, nigga! My fuckin' brother! You think I'm just gon' let that shit slide? Huh?"

"Nah, I don't."

"Aight then. I had to bury my fuckin' brother over this shit!"

I shrugged. "Better him than us."

My finger closed around the trigger before squeezing it. Blood drained from his head and chest onto the carpet. Once the last shell hit the ground, everything went silent. There was bloodshed all around me, but I wasn't finished. I wanted that mothafucka's body to desiccate. When his niggas couldn't find his body, that's when they'd get the message. BBG and the Blackwell boys didn't fuck around.

I stepped out of the house with his dead body in tow. The city streets were wet with fresh snow as it fell from the sky. I tossed his body in the trunk and started the car to take him to his final resting place: a greasy dumpster behind a fast-food restaurant downtown. The smell of his rotting body would fit right in with the rotting garbage smell that hung in the alleyway.

I drove my car down the dark alley and got out. Graffiti covered the mildew stains on the brick walls as I shuffled over crushed boxes of Chinese takeout and thousands of cigarette butts underneath my feet. I stepped in a greasy-looking puddle before tossing his body into the dumpster and closing the top so the rats and roaches could feed off him. Nobody was gon' fuck with us anymore.

"Rest in pieces, mothafucka."

As soon as everything was done, I pulled out my phone to call Frenchie. I could smell the gun oil on my fingertips as I held the phone to my ear. Instead of hearing his voice on the other end, I heard Elite's. "He's sleep, P," she whispered to me.

"Aight. Tell him I'll call him in the morning."

"Did you uh, take out the trash?" she asked.

"I did." I nodded.

She paused. "Good... Thank you f—for everything."

"Anytime, anyplace," I assured her and ended the call.

Chapter Thirteen

ELITE

A week passed since Frenchie had been released from the hospital. Minus the limp he had when he walked, it was as if he was almost back to normal. Until we were able to find a new place to live, we were staying in Pharaoh's basement, which was the size of a luxury apartment. It seemed like when I got Frenchie back home, Paxton and Imani both got colds. I was juggling waiting on a household of broken and sick people, while also making sure my business was running smoothly. On the outside, I looked like Superwoman, but on the inside, I felt like I was going to lose my damn mind.

Imani was sitting on the couch, coloring, with a low-grade fever, while I had Paxton in my arms, feeding him before giving him his second dose of medicine. Frenchie came downstairs and walked into the kitchen to take his pain medication.

"Give him to me," he said.

"Nah, it's okay. I got him. He'll go to sleep soon."

"You look tired, Elite. Give 'em to me. I got him. You go take a shower and lay down."

"Are you sure?"

"They my kids too, ain't they? I got it."

I passed Paxton over to him and watched him kiss his forehead. He limped over to the other couch and rocked him in his arms while watching TV. He made it look so easy. Before I walked into the room, I heard a knock on the back door.

"I got it," I told him.

"Yo, Elite. Chill. I got it. It's just Corinne dropping off Junior."

I shrugged one shoulder. "Oh, okay."

With Paxton in his arms, I watched him walk over to the door to open it. Corinne and Junior walked in holding hands, while I stood off to the side.

"Hi, Daddy!" Junior said, wrapping his arms around Frenchie's waist.

He bent down to kiss his forehead. "Hey, Junior."

"Hey, I don't mean to interrupt, but I just thought you should know that both the kids are sick. They are taking medicine, but if Junior winds up with a cold, he more than likely got it from one of them," I told Corinne.

"Thanks," she said dryly.

Frenchie looked at me and grabbed my hand before I could turn to leave. "Look, now that I got everybody here, I just wanted to make some shit clear going forward."

"Like what?" Corinne asked.

"First thing's first, respect. Don't be showin' up at her job no more on some bullshit. If you got somethin' to address with me, then address it with me. Don't go out and put our shit in the streets. Elite is my girl, and she's runnin' her business with no drama, aight?"

She folded her arms across her chest. "So y'all back together now?"

I looked at Frenchie, and he looked back at me. "Yeah, we are workin' it out, right, Elite?"

I nodded slowly. "Yeah."

"So going forward, anything between me and you is dead. All I care about is the well-being of my son."

She had a sour look on her face as she bobbed her head up and down. "Wow. A nigga get shot up, and all of a sudden he's brand new."

"Fuck all that. I should've been said this shit to you, but I was bein' selfish. I'm tryna do right by everybody in my family this time around, aight? You ain't gotta like the shit, just respect it."

"Whatever, Frenchie. I'll call you before I come pick him

up in a few days," she said before turning to leave.

"Wow," I said in shock.

"What?"

"What made you do all of that?"

"Like I told her, I should've been did that shit. When I told you I wanted my family back when I was laying in that hospital bed, I meant every word of that shit."

I could feel myself welling up with emotions, but all I could do was nod. I backed away from him to go take a shower, when he stopped me.

"Elite, hold up. There's something I've been wanting to talk to you about."

"What is it?" My shoulders tensed, hoping he wouldn't say anything that would piss me off.

"I just wanted to say thank you."

"For what?"

"For everything..."

"You're welcome, Frenchie."

"Imani, why don't you show Mommy the picture you drew for her?"

"Okay, Daddy!"

She crawled off the couch and walked over to hand me a picture with five stick figures on it, representing the four of us and her brother Junior. "Aww, it's so pretty, baby girl. Thank you."

"Turn it over."

I flipped the paper over, and in big, colorful letters read the words 'say yes.' "Say yes? Yes to what, Imani?"

"To me," Frenchie said, slowly getting down on one knee.

"Oh my God!" I yelled as I fanned my cheeks, wet from tears of surprise and happiness.

"All my life I've been afraid of commitment, and we know that I'm no good at this love shit, but I promise that I'm trying to get better. You've seen me at my worst and my best, and you're still here. I've tried to let you go, and I can't. You're the total package, Elite, and I want to make what we built work for us this time. Believe me when I tell you that I don't want anyone else but you."

My eyes lit up as fresh tears dominated my face. I couldn't believe he was giving me the proposal I'd always dreamed of. It was heartfelt. It was real. It was everything I'd ever wanted. It was one of the first times that I could see the man I'd fallen in love with seven years ago, finally resurfacing.

"Elite, will you marry me?" he asked.

I nodded as I swiped the tears away from my eyes. "Yes, baby. Yes, I'll marry you!"

His eyes lit up as he slid the ring onto my finger and slowly climbed to his feet. I wrapped my arms around his neck and kissed him.

"Mommy and Daddy are getting married, Imani!" I squealed.

"Yay!" She clapped.

SAVANNAH

Pharaoh and I laid together, wrapped in his sheets, talking about everything from A to Z. I was so happy to have him back in my life.

"So it's your turn to tell me about you," he said.

"What else do you want to know?"

"Anything you haven't told me. Nah, you know what, fuck that. I want to know something that you've never told anyone before."

I cleared my throat as my heart rate started to quicken. Normally, the thoughts that were in my head would've never crossed my mind long enough for me to play around with the idea of expressing them. "I don't think you're ready to be thrown down the rabbit hole of my past."

"I thought we said no secrets."

"We did."

"Then what's so bad that you can't tell me?"

I wrapped the sheets tightly around my naked body, while pulling myself up on my elbows. "Well, my parents divorced when I was two years old. When she went back to her maiden name, she went through the process of getting my name changed, too, so that's how I went from Savannah Baptiste to Savannah McKinney."

"Whatever happened to your pops?"

I shrugged. "Last I heard, he was in jail."

"Jail? For what?"

"Dealin' drugs."

"Damn, fuckin' with drug dealers must be in ya blood," he joked.

"Shut up. That's why my mother left him. She didn't want me growin' up in that life."

"So you don't talk to him at all?"

"No. What do I have to say? I haven't laid eyes in him in over twenty years. He's a stranger to me."

"What's his name?"

"Why?"

"Tell me his name. I want to know."

"Vernon Baptiste."

He shrugged. "Never heard of him."

"Yeah, well that's my secret."

"I don't know why you're trippin' over this. It's not that big of a deal."

"It is to me. You remember I used to work for the FBI, right? I didn't want any ties to that life jeopardizing my job."

"And look at you now, naked in a drug dealer's bed."

"Shut up!"

"I'm joking with you. Don't worry about none of that shit from your past, Savannah. You with a real one now. I got you."

"There's something else I've been meaning to talk to you about."

"What?"

"The night that you shot Shep... You didn't kill him, you know?"

"Yeah, I know."

"You do?"

"If I wanted him dead, he'd be dead."

"Then why'd you shoot him?"

"To make him wish he was."

"Why didn't you shoot me?"

"I thought about it."

"I know. I could see it in your eyes that you wanted to, but why didn't you?"

"Because I loved you even then, and as mad as I was at

you, I didn't want to see anything happen to you."

Chapter Fourteen

SIX MONTHS LATER
ELITE

Frenchie and I had made it to see our wedding day come to fruition. I was incredibly nervous to start my forever with him, but I had loved Frances Blackwell since the moment I met him; nothing was going to change that. I stared at my reflection in the mirror, admiring the frills and lace on my ivory wedding dress with a crimson waistband. My fingertips ran down my thighs, feeling the ridges from the crystals all over the front of the dress.

"C'mon, Elite. It's time," my mother told me before she picked Paxton up. I leaned in to kiss him before sliding on my satin heels.

"Are you ready, baby girl?" I asked Imani, who had on a dress that almost mirrored mine.

"Yes!" she cheered.

"Pick up your basket of flowers, and let's go. It's almost time to go see Daddy."

The long train of my floor-length ball gown followed behind me as we made our way to the sanctuary doors.

"I love you, Mommy," she said before she walked in to drop rose petals on the ground.

"I love you more," I whispered.

Dru Hill's "I Do" started playing as I entered the sanctuary holding the crimson bouquet of roses with sprouts of baby's breath tight in my grasp. My eyebrows knitted together as happy tears swam out of my eyes the moment I caught Frenchie's eyes. I was staring a little too long at him that I almost forgot to keep walking. There were no words to describe the feelings I felt as my eyes scanned the people around me. Each of my bridesmaids looked gorgeous in their crimson red gowns, and all the guests were wearing smiles.

"Who gives this bride to be married?"

I looked over at my mother who was holding Paxton. She stood. "I do."

"If anyone has just cause as to why these two should not form their everlasting union today, speak now or forever hold your peace." The room fell silent, and he continued. "Ladies and gentlemen, we have all gathered here before God and one another to celebrate the union of Frances—"

"Frenchie," he said, cutting him off.

"To celebrate the union of Frenchie and Elite. You may now be seated."

He looked at both of us and continued. "Frenchie and Elite, you two have been together for seven years. Through the course of your relationship, you two have endured your shares of ups and downs, but it is the strength of your love that has brought you two here today. Amen?"

"Amen," the crowd replied in unison.

"You two have chosen to go down the path of marriage as one. To continue down this path, it's going to take the three T's, which are trust, truth, and time. If you are ready to embark on this journey together, reply 'we do,'" he said.

"We do," we said in unison.

"Okay, now it is time for the vows. The bride and groom have elected to recite their own vows. Elite, when you're ready, you may go ahead."

My lungs expanded then exhaled with nervous energy bouncing around in them. I placed both of my hands in his and looked into his dark brown eyes. "Frenchie, baby, we've been riding this roller coaster of life together for seven years now, and over those years, I've learned what it means to love you through the pain. I've learned what it means to love you through the good and the bad. I know that every day of our forever together won't be easy, but I promise to do my part and continue to nurture and cherish your heart. From the moment

I met you, it's been you, and it's going to always be you. You've given me two children who are the best parts of me, and you did what you had to do to make sure than our family remained intact. You've worked overtime to put the pieces of my heart back together, and for that, I thank you. I love you, and I'm ready to spend the rest of my life right beside you."

"Under the eyes of God, do you take her to be your lawfully wedded husband?"

"I do."

"Now take the ring and place it on his finger."

FRENCHIE

I ran my hands over my beard as I looked into Elite's eyes. She looked like an angel straight out of heaven. The pastor looked at me and nodded. "Frenchie, you may recite your vows now."

I drew in a deep breath as I reached out and swiped a loose curl ringlet behind her ear. "Elite, I never knew real love until I met you. You're my medicine when I'm sick. My smile when I'm frowning. You make me happy in a way that no one else can. You are the center of my whole world. Everything I do, say, or feel begins and ends with you. I know that these past few years with me haven't been the easiest, but I promise that you are my one and only today, tomorrow, forever. I just want to thank you for saving me when I was lost. For that, I'll love you until I take my very last breath."

"Under the eyes of God, do you take her to be your lawfully wedded wife?"

"I do."

"Now take the ring and place it on her finger."

I slid the ring on her finger and smiled.

"Frenchie and Elite, before today, you were two individuals living life. From this day forward, you are one. The good lord has blessed you with beautiful children, and now your love has brought your family closer. We have all witnessed the commitments and promises you've both made to each other. And I could not be happier than to say this next line. By the power vested in me and the state of Illinois, I now pronounce you husband and wife. Frenchie, you may salute your bride."

I pulled her lips onto mine as the crowd cheered, and applause filled the sanctuary. "I love you," I whispered against her lips.

"I love you, too."

"Ladies and gentlemen, it is my honor to introduce to you for the very first time, Mr. and Mrs. Frances Blackwell!"

Chapter Fifteen

PHARAOH

Imani and Junior ran between the tables, playing tag, while Elite's mother held onto Paxton. Elite and Frenchie entered, and everyone cheered, hollered, and whooped. They made their way over to the head table, hand in hand. He leaned in to kiss her, and I smiled. It took a lot for Frenchie to realize the error of his ways and turn his shit around, but I was glad he did. I knew how much Elite and his family meant to him, and I was glad that he was able to win everything back after losing it all.

After everyone had taken their seats, I rose from mine to make a toast. I held the champagne flute in my hand as I clinked the side of the glass with a gold knife. The room settled down, and I cleared my throat. "As the best man, they are tellin' me that I'm supposed to say a few words. So, to the bride and groom, congratulations to you both. French, even though you're older than me, it's been a privilege to watch you grow and be a provider to your kids and now your wife. All the pain we done been through, you deserve this shit, nigga. I know Big Mama is lookin' down on all of this, and she's real proud right now. Cheers."

"Cheers!" everyone repeated and then drank their champagne.

"Aww, that was beautiful, P. Thank you!" Elite said as she came over to hug me.

"Congratulations again."

"Thank you."

"I'm about to go hit up this open bar that I paid for," I

joked.

"Best wedding gift ever!"

I headed over to the bar to get myself a drink and smiled to myself. Life was finally good again. There was no more drama between MCF and BBG. It wasn't a secret that if any nigga jumped out of pocket, we would be there to correct 'em. Imani was home. Frenchie and Elite were back together and married, and I landed a new connect and was still doing my thing while running the community center and starting the construction of another. Most importantly, things between Savannah and I were back at a place that I never thought we'd get to. I knew that not everyone deserved a second chance, but for the ones that did, I had to give it to them. I'd given them to both Frenchie and Savannah, and they hadn't disappointed me since.

With my drink in my hand, I walked over to the table where Savannah was sitting and kissed her cheek. "Hey, beautiful."

She looked at me and smiled. "Hey yourself."

"So I've been thinkin'…"

"About what?"

"You, me… this whole living situation, and I came to the conclusion that it's time for a permanent change in location."

"For you?"

"No, you."

"What are you saying, Pharaoh?"

"I'm sayin'… we've been doin' this back and forth thing for a while now, and I think we should both just say fuck it, and you go ahead and move in with me."

I searched her eyes for any hesitation and couldn't find any. I knew my proposition must have come as a surprise to her. We'd never talked about moving in together, and before Savannah, I never even thought about cohabitating with another female for more than a night. It had gotten to the point where I needed her to be the first person I saw in the morning when I woke up and the last person I saw at night. Savannah was the love of my life, and since she was back in my life, I was going to do everything in my power to make sure she stayed for good.

SAVANNAH

The entire reception buzzed with conversation from all the guests. Even with all the people around me, I couldn't take my eyes off Pharaoh. I couldn't believe he'd asked me to move in with him. My insides were jumping for joy, but I tried to remain calm. I could always find a new career or place to live, but I would never find another man like Pharaoh Blackwell.

"So, what do you think?" he asked me.

"I think it's a yes."

"Yes?" he asked.

I nodded. "Yes, I'll move in with you."

His eyes creased as he smiled. I stood frozen, just taking in all of him. I'd never seen him in a suit before, and I was salivating like a dog. Every article of clothing on his body was custom fitted. The only time I allowed myself to break my eyes away from him was when I first got up to go congratulate the newlyweds. It amazed me how much love was radiating off of both of their bodies and filling up the room. Anyone with eyes could see how much in love those two were. With as much as they'd been through, they were still able to turn it all around and make it down the aisle. They were hood relationship goals, for real.

I turned my attention away from Pharaoh when the DJ called all the women to the dance floor to catch the bouquet.

"Go on out there. I'll be here when you get back," he told me.

"Are you sure?"

"Yeah."

He nudged me, and I made my way out to the floor, standing amongst the other ladies at the reception.

"Ready? One... two... three!" Elite heaved the bouquet over her head, and I watched it fly into the air. Her bridesmaids were clawing for it, when it landed right at my feet. I bent down to pick it up and locked eyes with Pharaoh.

"Wow..." I mumbled.

Elite looked at me and then back at Pharaoh with a smile on her face. "Watch out now."

She took her seat, and everyone crowded around as Frenchie slid the garter belt off her thigh. He stood and tossed it to all of the eligible bachelors standing behind him. I laughed when it landed right at Pharaoh's feet. He shook his head as the rest of the men around him whooped and hollered. His fingertips swiped it, and he swung it in circles around his index finger. The moment he locked eyes with me, I could've melted into a puddle right there on the dance floor.

Elite walked over to me and pulled me onto the chair so that Pharaoh could slide the garter belt onto my thigh. He walked over to me with a hellish grin written across his face. Before he dropped down to one knee, he leaned in and kissed my lips.

"Don't start moanin' in front of all these people when I get down there," he said.

I could feel my face turning red as he dropped down to one

knee and stretched the garter belt wide, then lifted my leg up to his shoulder. The onlookers in the crowd cheered and giggled, never able to take their eyes off us. Pharaoh's hands glided over my calf and up my thigh with ease until I felt the piece of fabric snap tightly around my leg. Everyone clapped as I pulled his lips onto mine in the middle of the floor.

"May I have this dance?" he asked, extending his hand to me.

I placed my hand in his and smiled wide. "Of course."

We moved the chair and stepped back out onto the dance floor with the other couples. Pharaoh pulled my body close to his and buried his lips in the nape of my neck. "You look gorgeous tonight," he whispered in my ear.

"Thank you, baby."

"Are you having a good time?"

"Yeah, I am. You?"

"Yeah. I can't believe I caught the bouquet."

"You know what that means, right?"

"That I'm supposed to be the one to get married next, right?"

"Yeah."

"So what do you plan on doing about that?" I asked him.

He shrugged with a devilish grin across his face. "I don't know… maybe one day."

I loved Pharaoh Blackwell with every breath in my body. He was as rare as they came. I rested my head against his chest, listening to his heartbeat, and smiled. We may have had a long way to go before we got the chance to have a wedding of our own, but I was going to enjoy every minute of my life with him. It was just the beginning for us.

The End

A Note from the Author

Reader,

Thank you for reading the finale of the *Fallin' for the Alpha of the Streets* series. Please, if you've made it this far, I hope you'll consider taking a minute to tell me what you thought about the book or the series as a whole in the form of a **book review**. Don't hesitate to let me know what you'd like to see from me next! I thoroughly enjoy reading your reviews and hearing from you as well! I'm always striving to attract new readers and retain current ones, and reviews are one of the easiest ways to attract readers. If you loved the book, tell a friend, and most importantly, let me know!

All my love,

KL Hall

About the Author

As a serial storyteller, K.L. Hall pens enthralling love stories intertwined with the grittiness of urban fiction. Her writing style is a fusion of eminently relatable female characters like Sydney Tate and Raquel Valentine, and the flawed, yet desirable male leads who love them, like Law Calloway and Justice Silva.

Highly Acclaimed Series:
In the Arms of a Savage: (Peaked at #1 in Women's Fiction)
In the Arms of a Savage 2: (Peaked at #3 in Women's Fiction)
In the Arms of a Savage 3: (Peaked at #2 in Women's Fiction)
Fallin' for the Alpha of the Streets: (Peaked at #4 in Women's Fiction)

Text KLHALL to 22828 to sign up for my mailing list to stay up to date with new releases, giveaways, sneak peeks and more! Connect with Me on Social Media:
Facebook: K.L. Hall https://goo.gl/yGP59B
Twitter: @authorklhall
Instagram: @authorklhall
Website: www.authorklhall.com

Other novels by K.L. Hall:
Diary of a Hood Princess 1-3
Rise of a Street King: The Justice Silva Story *(Spin-Off to the Diary of a Hood Princess series)*
Where He Belongs: A Disrespectful Love Story
Love Me Harder: A Sin City Love Story
Broken Condoms and Promises 1-3
In the Arms of a Savage 1-3

Built for a Savage: Blaze and Camille's Love Story *(Spin-Off to the In the Arms of a Savage Series)*
A Ruthle$$ Love Story 1-3
Fallin' for the Alpha of the Streets 1-2
The Most Savage of Them All: The Wolfe Calloway Story *(Prequel to the In the Arms of a Savage Series)*
When a Gangsta Loves a Good Girl

Novellas:
Bi-Curious: An Erotic Tale
House of Cards
A Savage Calloway Christmas *(Christmas novella to the In the Arms of a Savage Series)*
Lovin' the Alpha of the Streets: A Valentine's Day Novella *(Valentine's Day novella to the Fallin' for the Alpha of the Streets Series)*
Awakened: A Paranormal Romance Novella
Caught Between my Husband and a Hustler